CHAOS

AYANA N. WILLIAMS

Copyright © 2024 AYANA N. WILLIAMS
All rights reserved
First Edition

Fulton Books
Meadville, PA

Published by Fulton Books 2024

ISBN 979-8-89221-157-4 (paperback)
ISBN 979-8-89221-158-1 (digital)

Printed in the United States of America

CHAPTER

1

New Chapter

I was so excited about completing my degree! And I finally received my CPA. Now I was looking forward to starting my own company. For now, my plan was to work at this accounting firm in Downtown Houston, Texas, until I could do that!

Scratching my head, I looked over at the time. It was 7:15 p.m., and I am still at work.

"Ha! I have no life," I said that aloud to no one. Thank God the office was empty, or they would all think that I was crazy.

Logging off my computer, I grabbed my purse, briefcase, and jacket and headed to the elevators. I was trying to run out of there! It was Friday, and I was looking forward to doing nothing but scratching my butt all weekend. I giggled at that thought.

My phone rang and scared the shit out of me. Damn, it was my cousin Victoria, or Vicki, which was what I lovingly called her. Every time she called, I had to listen to her beg me to do something. "Let's go party, Maya. Let's go to the club, Maya. Let's go to the mall, Maya." Hell no!

"Hello?"

"It's Friday, Maya!"

"Yes, Vicki. I am aware of that." All I could hear was music in the background, which made me speak loudly into the phone.

"Vicki, turn your music down! I can't hear myself speak!"

"Okay, okay, girl!"

I waited for her to sing an off-key version of "Climax" by Usher. After it seemed like she sang the whole song, she finally turned the music down.

"Hey, Maya, do you want to go to this party with me tonight?"

"Come on, Vicki. Last time I went to a party with you, the cops came. I'm not with that mess tonight, or ever."

"It's a party over in the Woodlands. This lawyer dude is throwing the party."

"I don't know, Vicki."

"Come on, Maya, please. I want to hang out with my big cousin this weekend."

"Shit, Vicki, I just want to lie around and watch movies all weekend."

"That's all you ever do! You need to get out of the house. One of these days, you are going to have to let me hook you up with this—"

"Oh, hell no, Vicki, that will never happen!" I yelled, interrupting that crap coming out of her mouth. "Last time I let you hook me up, dude stalked me for a month. I had to go down to the courthouse to get that shit to stop!"

"Whatever! Mike really liked you. Anyway, just go with me for an hour. If you don't like the vibe, then we can leave. Please, Maya?"

I sighed. Putting my head down into my hand, I shook it quickly. "Damn, okay."

"Okay, cousin, I will pick you up at 9:30!" She hung up before I could respond, which was very typical of my cousin.

I got home and took a shower and stood in the closet and tried my best to find something to wear.

My phone rang, and I ran to catch it.

"Hello."

"Maya?"

"Yes, Vicki?"

"Wear something sexy. Don't be trying to put on one of your little uptight suits that you wear to work. That shit is not cute!" *Click.*

That girl hung up on me again.

"Ugh!" Shaking my head, I made my way back to the closet.

I picked out a black off-the-shoulder dress that came above the knee and some black pumps. I pulled my natural hair up into a bun and pulled a long section of it out to hang to the left of my face. Simple diamond stud earrings with a matching necklace and bracelet completed my outfit.

The doorbell rang just as I was walking down the steps.

I opened the door, and my full-of-life cousin grabbed me and hugged me. "Hey, boo! You ready? Ooh, cousin, I love that dress! I didn't know you had shit like that in your closet. Ha!"

"Hey, girl. Yeah, I am as ready as I will ever be, and very funny, Vicki. Let's go before I change my mind."

My cousin had on a little, tight, spaghetti-strap red dress, with some cheetah-print pumps and a matching purse.

"Nice dress, Vicki."

"Thanks, cousin!"

We had our little catch-up conversation on the way there, and it got a little quiet. I could tell that she had something to say. She kept nervously glancing over at me.

"What, Vicki?"

"Yo, cousin, I just don't like that you don't come out of your house. You go to work, go home, go to church, and go to the store. That's it! You really need to get out more. Cousin, that shit is not cool," she said, shaking her head before focusing back on the road and lightly patting my arm.

I sighed. I knew she was right. But I just finished school three months ago. I was enjoying the downtime before things really took off with my business.

"I know, cousin. I will try and do better. But I will not do crazy parties or anything like that with you. I don't like all that extra, Vicki. You know you can get too wild, and I cannot hang with you like that."

"Okay, okay. I promise no more crazy parties or whatever. But, girl, you ever thought about getting you a man? Shit, maybe you would relax more. I'm just saying, cousin! What harm could it do?"

"I am good. I am not for those games. And I definitely don't like getting my heart broken. I had enough of that with the last guy I was dating."

"Damn, Maya, that was two years ago."

"I know how long ago that was, thanks. When I'm ready for a *man*, then it will happen. I am not in any big hurry for all that." I rolled my eyes at her, and she giggled. I smiled and shook my head.

We finally pulled up to this huge house. My cousin gave the keys to the valet, and we walked to the front door and rang the doorbell.

A man opened the door and asked us for our names. He found my cousin's name and quickly stepped aside and opened the door to let us in.

I was so impressed by this house. It was like something out of a magazine. There was a beautiful stairway to the right in the foyer. A very beautiful and very huge kitchen and dining area sat off to the right of the entry. We walked toward the back of the house and into a huge room. It looked like it might be the living room. There were so many people there, but not too many where we couldn't move around. Glancing around, I took note of the beautiful decorations, drapes, and wood flooring as far as the eye could see. Marble counters and stainless-steel appliances in the kitchen. It was a very beautiful home.

"Look, girl! There's my friend Terrance. This is his house, his party." She yanked me over to him.

"Hey, Terrance, how are you? Nice house!" my cousin yelled as Terrance pulled her in for a hug.

"I'm good, Vicki. Where is your boyfriend? I invited you both."

He was talking to my cousin but looking at me from head to toe like he wanted to eat me. I suddenly felt uncomfortable and reached around and began to scratch the back of my neck.

"Yeah, I know. He had to work. He said he will try and get here a little later. Oh, Terrance. This is my cousin, Maya. The one I was telling you about." When she said that, I turned and gave her a dirty look. It was like me telling her that I didn't want to be fixed up with anyone went in one ear and came out the other. I didn't need a matchmaker. It took everything in me not to curse her out as I frowned at her.

"Hello, beautiful," Terrance said as he grabbed my hand and kissed it while placing his other hand on my shoulder.

"Hello. You have a very beautiful home," I said as I quickly pulled my hand from his and wiped it on my dress and stepped aside so that his hand would fall from my shoulder.

"Thank you very much, Maya. Please make yourself at home. I need to make sure things are going smoothly. Please save me a dance, beautiful," he said as he grabbed and kissed my hand again and walked away. He was fine. I have to give it to him. But I wasn't interested, I thought as I wiped my hand again on my dress.

I waited until he walked away then turned to my cousin. "Vicki! Dammit! What did I say?" I loudly whispered to her, hoping not to cause a scene.

"I am not trying to play matchmaker. Well, maybe I am. He is a nice guy, Maya. Damn, relax. Loosen up."

"I don't give a shit, Vicki. See, now I feel like it's time for me to leave."

"Please, cousin, we just got here. Give it an hour," she whined. I shook my head and let out a breath. Never again, I thought, getting frustrated at the whole scene.

Turning, I walked past her without another word and walked farther into the room. Standing by the patio and looking out to the pool, I scanned the whole area. Beautiful brown and gold tables and lounge chairs. The water was a beautiful blue, and there was a Jacuzzi and small waterfall in the center.

Spotting Terrance hugging and flirting with two ladies, I frowned and began to get disgusted. One of them grabbed him between his legs. The other grabbed a handful of his ass. He looked over in my direction, and his smile faded. I shook my head and walked away from the door and over by the buffet table, where I focused on the mounds of food displayed along that one stretch of wall. There was so much food. I made myself a small plate of catfish and a salad. Quickly scanning the room, I spotted an empty seat at the bar, and I took it.

I ate my food and slowly looked around, taking in the beauty of the home. A lot of guys were looking my way, smiling. I rolled my eyes and turned my back and continued eating.

"There you are, beautiful. I've been looking all over for you."

"Ha! That's funny, Terrance. Somehow, I doubt you were looking for me," I said, never looking at him. I looked everywhere but at him.

"Would you like to dance, Maria?"

Chuckling, I shook my head. "No, thanks, Terrance. And my name is Maya." I got up from the bar and quickly headed over to my cousin. "I'm leaving, Vicki."

"Okay, girl. This party is boring. Let's go. Girl, why is Terrance looking at you like that?"

"Well, he called me Maria and asked me to dance. I politely told him no and reminded him that my name is Maya and walked away from him. Humph, he can look all he wants." I shook my head at him as we walked out the door.

"Okay, girl. Do you want to stop and get something to eat?"

"Yeah, that's fine. Let's go to IHOP. I want some pancakes."

"Maya, you eat like a pig and never gain any weight. Ooh, you make me sick!"

When we pulled up at IHOP, I was so happy that the place wasn't packed.

I ordered the breakfast sampler with the harvest grain and nut pancakes. My cousin ordered the same.

The waitress took our drink orders and walked away.

"So how are you and your boo? Y'all engaged yet?"

"Girl, you are so funny. No, we are not engaged. I don't know if either of us are ready for that yet."

"Hmm, okay, Vicki."

"What does that mean?"

"Oh, girl, nothing at all. I know how much you love Derrick. Don't settle if he is not making you happy. You deserve the best, and you know you do."

"Thanks, cousin. He is good to me. Yes, I do love him. But I just want to make sure first. Know what I mean?"

"Yeah, I do."

"Maya, I love you, but I don't want you to be bitter and alone like my mom. That's why I'm always on you to get yourself a man."

"I know. Believe me, I don't take it personal. I love you too. But the last guy I was with hurt me to the core. I am just now able to finally forgive and move on. I have a peace about it now. I forgave him, and now I just want to work on me. I am not ready for a relationship yet. In time, that will come. But for now, I am content with being by myself."

"I know, Maya. I hate that he hurt you like that. When you told me that he cheated on you, well, that hurt me too. You didn't deserve that. No one does."

"Anyway, girl, enough of that mess. I am not trying to be all depressed," I said as I waved a hand.

I looked away from her and out the window. I didn't want her to see the tears in my eyes. Yes, I was healed from that, and I was moving on. But that relationship took a lot out of me. I gave so much of me, sacrificed a lot for that relationship, only to get hurt so badly.

The waitress brought our food. We were both silent as we ate, and I was glad for the silence. It allowed me to quickly collect myself.

"Okay, Vicki, let's go. Are you staying at my house tonight, or are you going home?"

"Oh, girl, I'm going home. My boo is there, waiting for me."

"Okay. I understand. Go on and get you some. I am definitely not mad at you."

We rode to my house in silence. I nodded off a few times, but we finally pulled into my driveway.

I hugged my cousin before getting out of her car. "Call me so that I know you made it home, Vicki."

It was 1:00 a.m. by the time I had taken a shower and put my hair up. I was wired and didn't think that I would be able to sleep. I decided to head downstairs and find a movie and fix a quick snack. I chose *Love Jones*, and homestyle popcorn covered in red-dot hot sauce, a bag of pistachios, and a glass of ice water. So much salt, I know, but it had been a while since I had indulged in my favorite snack.

While on my way up the stairs, the phone rang, and I almost tripped trying to get to it.

"Hello?"

"Hey, Maya, I made it home. Love you, girl, and I will talk to you tomorrow. Oh, well, it's already tomorrow. I will talk to you later."

"Good night, Vicki. Glad you made it home. I love you too, cousin."

I started the movie and got comfortable on my big pillows and started eating my snack. *Love Jones* was one of my favorites.

I didn't remember when the movie ended or when I fell asleep.

CHAPTER 2

Shouldn't Have Happened

I was jolted out of my sleep by the ringing of the doorbell. I glanced over at the clock, and it read 10:28 a.m. Wow, I slept a little later than usual. The doorbell rang again, and I slowly pulled myself out of bed and slowly *thumped, thumped* down the steps.

Looking out of the peephole, I saw that it was Vicki.

"What the hell," I said as I swung the door open. "Whatever it is, Vicki, the answer is no. Go away, I'm tired!"

"Hey, cousin, get your ass up. Go shower, brush your teeth, and get some clothes on. We have been invited to a beach party."

"Girl, spare me please. Vicki, I have not had my coffee or breakfast or anything. I don't feel like hanging out. I wanted to lie around the house all day. Why didn't you call me first before you came over?"

I slammed the door after Vicki walked through, and I stood with my hands on my hip and gave her an ugly face. She quickly shot me the finger and rolled her eyes at me.

"I didn't call because I know you, Maya. You would have said no. You always say no to fun. Let's get it, girl! Party starts at three. Chop-chop!" And to emphasize the chop-chop, Vicki smacked me on the arm and pushed me toward the stairs.

"Vicki, I need some coffee and to get myself together." I turned from the stairway and headed for the kitchen determined to get some coffee and something to eat.

She followed me to the kitchen and was going on and on about who knew what. I was not awake yet and hadn't had any coffee. My brain was not trying to process anything she had to say.

Taking the pan out, I proceeded to make a bagel sandwich using a whole-grain bagel, eggs, turkey bacon, and low-fat cheddar cheese. I didn't need to ask; I already knew Vicki hadn't eaten, so I made her one too.

"Girl, did you hear me?"

"Shit, no, Vicki. What did you say?"

"I asked if you had a swimsuit, a sexy swimsuit. Not something from the 1970s. Stop covering up your goodies and show them!"

"Shut up. Why are you so loud? Yes, I have a swimsuit. I have several. Let me wake up! Please." After I said it, we both paused and busted out laughing.

We sat and ate our bagels and drank coffee in silence. I was flipping through the newspaper, and Vicki was playing games on her phone.

We both looked up at the same time.

"I don't know, Vicki. After that party last night, I am having second thoughts about hanging out with you."

"Ugh, I forgot to tell you. Terrance called Derrick this morning, asking about you. I don't know what you did, but he begged Derrick to get you two together. And you don't have to give me that look. I told him that you were not interested. But don't be surprised if Derrick calls you himself. He seems to think that you two would be good together."

"Damn, I wish you two would stop trying to play matchmaker. Terrance is not my type. When I first saw him, I was thinking how fine he was. But after I saw him out by the pool with those girls, and then he forgot my name. I lost interest. I've dated men like him before. I promised myself that I would not do it again."

"Okay. Let's change the subject. Are you going to the beach party or not?"

"I really don't want to go anywhere, Vicki. Not sure why you can't get that through your big head. Where is it located?"

"Whatever, Maya. You are so moody in the morning. It's at Derrick's parents' house. They are doing a beach themed BBQ in the backyard by the pool. It should be fun. Derrick's mom asked me to invite you. She seems to think that you and Daren should be together."

"Seems like everyone is all up in my love life. Really, all of you need to get some new business and get far away from mine. Of course, I will go. I love Mr. and Mrs. Clark and wouldn't mind hanging out over there with them. Let me go shower and get dressed. Are you coming upstairs with me?"

"Yes, I need to approve of your outfit," she said, giggling.

I smacked Vicki on the arm, and we headed upstairs, talking about the day, laughing like school kids.

When we arrived at the Clark home, we had to find a place to park and ended up parking a street over. My stomach was in knots. I did not like crowds of people.

When we walked in the house, every face was familiar, so I quickly relaxed and started hugging and saying hi to everyone.

Daren was standing in the foyer, smiling at me, mouth wide open. Once I pulled away from my conversation with his aunt, he walked over to me.

"Hi, baby," he said and pulled me in for a big embrace and a kiss on the forehead.

Daren made me nervous. He has had a little crush on me since I was little. He was handsome, had a good job, very well-liked and known. But I just didn't feel the attraction to him that he felt for me. I must admit, though, he had a nice body—thick in all the right places—I thought as I squeezed him back.

"Daren, it's good to see you. Where are your parents?" I said and quickly pulled from his embrace.

I saw a look come over his face, but just as quickly, it was gone.

"Mom is in the kitchen, and Dad is outside on the grill." Grabbing my hand, he led me to the kitchen.

"Mom, look who's here."

His mom was bent over, pulling a pan from the oven. She turned and saw me, and a huge smile came across her face. My smile widened, and I walked toward her. I had to yank my hand from Daren's because he was holding it tightly, glancing at him and frowning as I walked away.

She was a tall, thick woman, with beautiful skin and hair. She had beautiful hazel eyes. Both her sons got their eyes from her.

Mrs. Clark hugged me like she hadn't seen me in years.

"Maya baby, why you don't come around to visit us anymore? We do miss you and would love to see you more often." Her voice was sort of husky and deep.

"I know, and I am sorry, Mrs. Clark. I had gotten so busy with school. I know that is not an excuse, and I promise you and Mr. Clark will see me more often. Can I help you with anything?"

"No, baby. Enjoy yourself. Go have fun. I will see you later."

"Yes, ma'am."

"Can I talk to you for a minute, Maya?"

"What's up, Daren?" I already knew what he wanted to talk about—what he always wanted to talk about—a relationship with me. And my answer would be like all my previous answers, no to the twelfth power.

"Follow me. I need to speak to you in private."

He led me up the stairs to the room his father used for an office. When I walked inside, he quickly closed the door.

I quickly scanned the room, and my skin crawled. His father had always kept this room a mess. I frowned, looking around at the clutter, and almost tripped on a stack of books. Daren grabbed me to steady me then let me go when I started pulling from him.

"What's up, Daren?" I said, anxious to get out of that room and back downstairs.

"Maya, we have known each other since we were little. I am at a point in my life where I really want to settle down. I've always wanted you to be in my life. I would like. No, let me back up. I would love to start a relationship with you. What do you think?" He smiled as if he had done something so big that deserved an award. His hazel eyes sparkled, and he cocked his head to the side, waiting for my answer.

For a second, my heart softened to him. As I looked into his hazel eyes, I felt something. I wasn't sure what it was. Maybe I felt sorry for him. I wasn't sure how to answer his question. I never thought about him in that way. I felt a little nervous and started looking around the room.

"Um, Daren. I don't know. I feel like this is the wrong time for this. I don't know. I feel put on the spot. Honestly, Daren, I've never thought of you that way. I've always looked at you as a good friend, kind of like a family member. This feels a little awkward. It's like you keep coming at me with this, and it's gotten redundant. I'm tired of telling you no," I said and headed toward the door.

I was feeling uncomfortable since he had closed the door and he was leaning against the door with his arms crossed. His face was now hard, with what appeared to be anger, hazel eyes now dark. There was no mistaking the anger coming from him.

He stood from his lean on the door and walked a few paces to me, stopping me in my tracks. I took a step back because now he was too close.

"Maya, I understand. But maybe if we spend some time together, it will change how you think of me. If you still feel the same way, then I will back off. What do you think?"

I relaxed. His face quickly softened. Hope framed his face. His hazel eyes were no longer dark. Just that quick, his anger was gone.

"Well, it couldn't hurt. I guess we could hang out sometimes. But honestly, that's all I can offer you."

"Thanks, Maya. I promise to be a gentleman." He smiled, dimples now prominent on his face.

We headed back downstairs, and I noticed Kiera walk in, and I thought, *Oh shit, trouble just blew in.*

She and I made eye contact, and she looked from me to Daren then rolled her eyes and went into the kitchen.

I chuckled at her display. She had been acting like a kid for as long as I could remember. I never knew what her problem was with me. But I didn't have time to ever entertain her. So I always kept away from her. Today was no different.

I looked at Daren, and he was smiling from ear to ear at me, and I didn't think he saw Kiera.

"Okay, Daren, I'm going to say hello to your father then find me a place to sit and eat," I said, putting a hand on his shoulder to stop his walk with me.

"I can go with you, baby," he said, putting his hand on the bare skin on my waist

"Daren, let's get this straight. We are friends. So calling me baby is not acceptable to me. Please don't call me baby. And I can say hello to your father without an escort." I smiled so that he wouldn't think that I was being rude.

He smiled, grabbed my hand, kissed it, and quickly walked to the kitchen.

Kiera was watching us. When he walked into the kitchen, she quickly pounced on him. She put on her big, stupid smile and walked to him and hugged him, cutting her eyes at me. He pushed her from him and turned toward me.

"Girl, get your ass off me!" His eyes got big when he realized that I was standing there, watching. He turned and started toward me.

I held my hand up and I shook my head and he turned and walked away from Kiera. She looked at him, walking away, and back at me.

"Dumbass," she said and shot me the finger.

"You are the only dumbass, Kiera. Grow up." I turned and quickly walked toward the patio door and outside. I wasn't going to let that bitch mess up my mood.

Daren's father was standing by a huge grill, talking to someone. I couldn't tell who it was because his back was to me.

"Hello, Mr. Clark, how are you doing? How have you been?" I said as I gently placed my hand on his arm to get his attention. The guy he was talking to turned, and I realized that it was Derrick.

"Hey, girl, what's up, Maya!" Derrick said as he shoved me.

We both laughed. He turned and walked off in the direction of my cousin, who was sitting on the side of the pool with her feet in the water, smiling in his direction.

"Come here and give me a hug. Where have you been? We never see you like we used to."

"I know, Mr. Clark. I am so sorry. I really don't have an excuse. I will do better. I promise to come see you and your beautiful wife more often."

"Okay, I will take your word for it, and all is forgiven. You want some meat off this pit?" Mr. Clark reached over and picked up a plate. "What do you want, the same as always? You want a sausage link, a turkey patty, chicken wings, and corn on the cob?"

"Ah, Mr. Clark, you remembered. That's it!" He reached me that plate and gave me a wink and turned toward the grill and started flipping hamburgers.

I looked around and spotted an empty seat and quickly walked toward it. Biting into my link, I was finally able to survey the party. I looked around and saw familiar faces, exchanging waves here and there. Lots of handsome men scattered in and around the pool. They all seemed to stop and stare as I walked by. I shook my head and tried to manage a small smile at a few then looked away. Some I didn't know, and some I did know. It seemed as if all eyes were on me, and I was uncomfortable.

I saw this tall, muscular chocolate man get up and walk toward my cousin once Derrick walked in the house. They laughed and both looked my way. They both waved, and I gave a quick wave and got up to walk into the house. I glanced his way and saw that he was watching me. I gave him a half smile and walked into the house. Looking toward the kitchen, I decided to keep my distance because Kiera was in there, laughing and talking loud to some ghetto bird.

I made my way into the family room. There were two older ladies sitting in there, watching TV, so I plopped on the sofa because it was empty. Before I knew it, I had nodded off. I didn't know how long I slept, but when I opened my eyes, Daren was sitting next to me.

"Hey, sweetheart, are you tired?"

"No, Daren. I guess the food put me to sleep." I felt uncomfortable because he was sitting so close to me, and he had his arm around the back of the couch.

I glanced at him and quickly stood and stretched. I noticed that we were alone in the living room.

"Maya, can I ask you something?" he said in a husky voice, a voice that made me frown but almost did something to me in that instance.

"Sure, what's up?" I said, wrapping my arms around my body. He was looking at me from head to toe, and it was making me feel uncomfortable.

"Can I kiss you? I mean, well, oh shit. I won't take it for more than it is. I won't make it into anything more than what it is either. I won't make a big deal out of it. But I really want to taste your lips," he said as he stood from his seat on the couch.

I stood there for a minute, staring at him. He had turned red in the face, and once he stopped talking, he looked down.

I slowly put my hand on my hip and took a step back. "Daren, I truly believe that if I gave you a kiss, you are going to do exactly the opposite of what you just said. You are going to make it more than it is. I don't have time for the extra. I told you that we could hang out, but I didn't say it came with extras."

He looked up, slowly making sure that he took in every curve of my body. His hazel eyes met mine, and he smiled. He slowly started walking toward me as he began to speak. I suddenly became uncomfortable. I lost my edge, and my arm dropped from my hip. The room suddenly got hot, and I started trying to back up and ended up against the wall.

He ran a finger down my arm as he smiled and licked his lips while staring at my lips. His hazel eyes had turned dark with desire. My breathing quickened the closer he got. He was so close I could feel his hot breath on my face. My body started failing me miserably and began to heat up from him being so close. My eyes were wide, and I began fidgeting and playing with my hair. I wasn't expecting these feelings from Daren being so close. Never thought he would make me so hot. But the way he was looking at me was getting to me.

He licked his lips and took my body in from head to toe again, stopping longer at my breasts, then he finally made his way to my face. He smirked and put one hand on the wall and leaned until our noses almost touched. He turned his face, and our lips almost touched. When he finally spoke, his voice was deep and husky. He ran his finger down my stomach, then he put his hand on my waist. I flinched and leaned my head back.

"Maya, I am not going to stand here and lie to you. I want you. I want to kiss you, suck on your neck, wrap my arms around your sexy body, and feel you pressed up against me. I want to hear you moan as I please you. I want to hear you say my name as I show you my love. I want to make love to you as you look into my eyes. I want to be sucking on your lips as your body quivers under me."

Suddenly I couldn't breathe. Daren broke the small distance we had between us. He leaned in and sucked my bottom lip. I didn't move, didn't stop him from doing it. I closed my eyes, and he grabbed me by my waist and pulled me to him. I got weak, and my knees almost buckled when he parted my lips with his tongue, and I took it in and gently sucked on it. I moaned, and he pressed his body into mine as he backed me into the wall. My eyes snapped open, and I stiffened. I was thinking how wrong this was. But it felt so good. My mind went in so many directions. Daren was a good friend, and I didn't want momentary weakness to wreck a lifetime friendship. Sensing my hesitation, Daren broke the kiss and looked in my eyes.

"Maya, please." He touched my cheek with his fingers and kissed my forehead, then down to my cheek. When he brushed his lips across mine, I lost all train of thought and gave in.

I wrapped my arms around his neck and pressed my body into his. He kissed me hungrily, and I fell deeper into his kiss. He grabbed my ass and pressed into me. He was rock hard and very big. The feeling of him pressing into me made me gasp, and I moaned as he grinded into me.

Daren slowly pulled his mouth from mine and kissed my cheek and down to my neck. He kissed my neck and lightly sucked on it. With his right hand, he cupped my left breast through my two-piece bathing-suit top. Sticking his hand under the top, he tweaked my nipple then leaned down to lick and suck on it.

I let out a moan, and my knees buckled, but Daren caught me and held me to him. He put one of my legs up, and I wrapped it around his body as he continued to grind into me.

"Y'all need to get a damn room! Nasty asses!" Kiera's voice was like nails on a chalkboard. I jumped and slid my leg back down to the floor.

I quickly regained my composure and straightened my bathing-suit top. Daren never looked from my face. He never turned around. He kept his eyes on me. The grinding had stopped, but he was still pressed up against me.

I realized that I was breathing hard, and I could feel wetness between my legs.

"Did y'all hear me?" Kiera screamed.

This time, we both turned to look at her.

"Go away, Kiera," Daren said to her.

She sucked her teeth and stomped off.

Daren turned and met my eyes. I looked away and realized that he was still pressed up against me. I could still feel him between my legs, and he started grinding in to me again, and I moaned.

"Please, Daren, stop," I said in a weak voice. I couldn't let this happen. I could feel our years of friendship slipping away. I couldn't let this happen. I loved him like family.

"Your mouth is saying one thing, Maya, but your body is saying something else. I know you want me just as much as I want you. Baby, all you have to do is say the word," he said as he kissed my neck then my lips again.

He stuck his hand down and under my sarong and through the side of my bikini bottoms and started rubbing on my swollen clit. I shuddered and moaned. Closing my eyes, I laid my head back on the wall then leaned forward and put my forehead on his shoulder.

"Daren, please, I can't do this. Please," I said as tears rolled down my face.

My body had betrayed me. I had promised that my heart had to be given first before I slept with anyone. But did it really matter with Daren? I had known him since I was little. He could take care of that itch. I hadn't been with anyone in two years. But while I was letting him scratch my itch, I would be breaking his heart and ruining a friendship. This sudden attraction to him had nothing to do with me wanting to be in a relationship with him but had everything to do with how horny I had been, how long it had been since a man had touched me.

Daren slowly backed away from me. He pulled his finger from my bikini bottoms and stuck it in his mouth. "Mm, Maya, you taste so good."

I adjusted my clothes and quickly walked away and toward the bathroom. Once inside, I sat on the toilet and put my head down in my hands. I didn't know how long I sat there, but I realized that I wasn't alone and quickly looked up and into the eyes of Daren. I didn't know when he came into the bathroom with me. I didn't hear a sound over my sniffles. Damn, I forgot to lock the door. Now here he was. My heart was beating fast, and I was ready to run through the wall and out the front door.

"Maya, I know that you aren't looking for a relationship. But maybe we can hang out from time to time and you can let me taste you. Let me please you, Maya."

"Daren, I know you. You would not be able to handle it. Your heart is so wide open, and I don't want to break it."

"Maya, just being able to please you is enough. If I feel like I am getting too deep, I promise I will back off. And I will let you know before I get too deep."

His eyes were pleading with me. I felt that, at any moment, he would drop to his knees and beg.

"Are you saying that you are okay with that, Daren? So what happens if, all of a sudden, I decide I want to be in a relationship, and I find someone, and that someone is not you? You do know that I won't be able to see you anymore? The sex would stop. And this could possibly ruin our friendship. And you are saying that you are okay with that too?"

"I'm not saying I'm okay with ruining our relationship, Maya. I just simply want to take us to another level. I think that whatever happens, we have known each other long enough not to let that ruin our friendship."

"Daren, another level, are you serious? You sound like a typical male now, and I'm not cool with that." Standing from my seat, I moved toward the door.

He wasn't listening, and I was tired of the begging.

"Maya, I am not trying to just sugarcoat shit so that I can get in your pants. I'm really not trying to do that. Damn, I feel like I'm begging. I've wanted you since as long as I can remember. This would allow me to have you all to myself when you allow it. I know we aren't in a relationship, and you aren't looking for that. I just really want to be with you."

He never faltered, but his eyes darkened—the darkening that seemed to send up red flags. That look that came over his face that made me question all the years I had known him. I didn't ever recall seeing this darkness in his eyes. It was in that moment that I should have said no. So many alarms were sounding off. But I didn't say anything.

"Can you give me some time to think about it, Daren?"

"Sure. But before I go, I want to leave you with something to think about."

The look in his eyes was intense. I decided right then that I needed an itch scratched, and if he thought that he could handle it, then so be it.

"What?" I said in a whisper as he pulled me to him.

Turning me around, he backed me against the bathroom door. I could feel the coldness on my bare skin, and I flinched. He sucked my bottom lip and licked the top. Just that quickly, he picked me up and put my legs around his neck. I felt a little wobbly for a second, up in the air, sitting with my pussy to his face. And just that quickly, he pulled my bikini bottoms to the side and licked my clit.

Weakness came over me, and if he wasn't holding me steady, I probably would have fallen. I moaned and grabbed his head for support. My body started shuddering from the touch of his tongue.

"Oh, shit," I breathed. Squeezing my legs together around his neck helped pull his face closer to me. I didn't care if I smothered him. I needed his face closer.

He sucked slowly, taking my clit into his mouth then making circles with his tongue then back to the sucking. And just that quickly, my body jerked. I pulled his head deeper into my heat as my body convulsed with waves of ecstasy. I turned and looked at us in the mirror. I couldn't see Daren's head because it was buried so deep into me.

His sucking got harder, and I felt myself starting to climax again. It was if he was draining all my energy from me. My body shook, and I bucked into his face. He started sucking slower as I rode the waves. I slowly grinded into his face, moaning, and held on to the back of his head for dear life. I could feel another wave coming, and I started grinding harder. His sucking got harder again, and I moaned and whispered his name over and over. I couldn't take any more, so I begged him to stop.

"Please stop. I can't take anymore." My voice was nothing but a whisper.

He slid me off his shoulders and stood me on my feet. When he let me go, I slid down to the floor.

He dropped his pants, and I gasped at how huge he was, and I got excited. I was ready to take all of him.

I managed to pull myself from the floor and walked over to him. Pushing him back toward the toilet, I made sure that he was in front of it.

"Sit down," I commanded. It was my turn to take him where he took me. "Do you have a condom, Daren?"

He pointed to his pants, and I walked over to them. "It's in my wallet" was the only thing that he could manage to say.

I pulled his wallet out and handed it to him. While he pulled the condom out, I dropped my bikini bottoms.

I noticed that the condom was a Magnum, and I smiled. He smiled at me as he rolled the condom down and over that thick and long piece of meat that looked like it was crooked.

I walked over to him slowly and watched how his eyes ran down my body. His hazel eyes turned dark, and he licked his lips. The darkness in his eyes this time was nothing but desire.

Slowly positioning myself over him, I slid down slowly over his manhood, making circles with my hips as I glided down. Daren moaned and grabbed my waist. I quickly pushed his hands away.

"I'm in control, Daren. Do. Not. Touch," I commanded and smirked at him.

He licked his lips and smirked back.

I started grinding up and down as I squeezed my muscles around his hard manhood. I could feel every inch of him and took him slowly so as not to cause pain. I made circles with my hips and alternated with the up-and-down grind.

Daren grabbed me and picked me up, with me still on him. He gently and swiftly laid me on the floor. The upper part of my body was on cold floor, and the rest of me was on a fluffy, soft rug. The cold floor was cooling my hot body down. I moaned, closed my eyes, and turned my head to the side.

He slowly kissed me as he pleased every inch and curve of my body. Wrapping my legs around his waist, I moved with each of his thrusts. Every thrust caused me to moan louder, and I quickly put my hand over my mouth and struggled to muffle my moans.

I could feel the waves coming, and I could feel him getting harder. The waves came, and I stopped my thrusts as I started bucking with the waves.

Daren stopped at the same time and held me tight as he and I came together, both breathing hard and softly, whispering the other's name.

Daren began to kiss me again, and I could feel him hardening again. I saw he had the same appetite that I had. If he didn't get all in his feelings, this should be fun. I smiled, ready for the next round.

He flipped me over and laid me on my stomach. I turned my head and watched as he pulled the already-used condom off and quickly put on another one. He laid his body on mine and quickly spread my legs wider. Kissing and licking on my neck, he settled into the curves of my body.

I felt that thick piece of meat enter me, and I moaned, forgetting to muffle myself. I turned my head, and we touched tongues then kissed passionately as he grinded slowly into me. Reaching around, he put his finger on my clit, and we slowly grinded until we both rode those waves again, me ending with an "Ugh."

Daren rolled from me and sat up. He reached over and put the other condom in the toilet then flushed.

We were both breathing hard and trying to regain some strength. I was looking at him, trying to catch his gaze, but he wouldn't look at me. *Oh shit, here we go.* I knew he wouldn't be able to handle this. I was regretting this. As amazing as this was, it wasn't worth the drama shit like this could bring. I turned my head away and closed my eyes.

I was the first to speak. "Daren, are you okay with this?" I said, not bothering to reopen my eyes and look at him.

It took him some time before he moved. He slowly looked up and met my eyes as I opened them. He had tears in his eyes, and one rolled down his face.

My mouth dropped open, and I sat up. "Daren, no, please don't do this."

"No, Maya. I'm not okay. I don't think that I will be okay with just being friends with you. That was intense and has deepened my feelings for you. So I will say this. If you ever decide that you want to let me love you the way you should be loved, I will be here. But I can't sleep with you again, baby. I thought that I could separate my feelings for you, but I can't. I think I love you more now than I ever did."

I slowly stood up. I didn't want to say any more to him. I felt used. I felt that he had lied just to get what he wanted. And like a dumbass, I gave it up and gave in to his begging. Opening the closet, I pulled out a towel and began to soap up a towel and clean myself. I couldn't look at him. I knew he was crying because I could hear him sniffing. After I got my clothes on and straightened my hair and fixed my makeup, I reached in the closet and got another towel down for Daren. Soaping it up, I handed it to him. He stood and took it and began to clean himself.

We never met eyes. I looked at the sadness in his face and turned to leave. I locked the door behind me and leaned my back against it. Listening for a minute, I heard him break down, his cries not loud but loud enough for me to hear his pain. My hand reached up, getting ready to knock, and I decided against it and walked away. I walked into the TV room, and Kiera was sitting on the couch.

"There you are, freak-nasty! Where is Daren?" She was frowning, and it appeared as if she had been crying. For a second, I felt sorry for her. But just that quickly, it was gone. I'd been the butt of too many of her remarks for too many years.

I wondered if she heard us. If she maybe stood by the door of the restroom as we did what we shouldn't have. I could see anger on her face, so I was guessing that she did. I was disgusted at her for doing what I wasn't sure she had done. I scowled at her angry face.

"I don't know, dumbass. Go find him yourself." Walking toward the patio door to head out to the pool, I stopped with my hand on the door. I stood, looking out for a second, trying to collect myself, trying to put on another face before walking outside.

As soon as I walked out, I looked toward Mr. Clark. "Hey there, young lady, what are you up to?" he said as I walked toward him. "Looking for more food, Maya?" he said and laughed.

"No, thank you, Mr. Clark. I came to see how you were doing and to see if you needed anything."

"No, I don't need anything. There is plenty of food, so make sure you fix you a plate before you leave here," he said, smiling at me then turning his face back to the smoking grill.

"Yes, sir, I definitely will. Thank you, Mr. Clark," I said as I lightly touched his arm and walked away.

Scanning the faces and waving at new people that had arrived, I finally spotted my cousin and started walking toward her. She was sitting in the corner with Derrick, and they were giggling. I didn't notice that that chocolate muscular man was sitting in the lounge chair next to them until it was too late for me to walk in another direction. Forgetting to not show any emotion, I rolled my eyes at him, smiling at me. His smile never faltered.

"There she is! Maya, where have you been? I wanted to introduce you to Phillip. Mr. Phillip Jackson, please meet my cousin, Maya Fontenot." I could tell she was drunk, and I frowned even harder. She was talking too loudly.

He stood from his seat, and I had to step back so that I could look up at him. He reached his hand out and shook my hand. He had large hands, and they swallowed mine.

"Maya, he has been smitten with you since we got here!" My cousin was clearly drunk, and people began to look our way. I frowned as I looked away from her and up at him.

"It's very, very nice to meet you, Maya." He had a very deep, smooth voice. Putting on a fake smile, I nodded my head.

"Nice meeting you as well, Phillip," I said and quickly let his hand go.

"There are no available seats, Maya, but you can share this seat with me."

"Thanks, Phillip," I said with a little more agitation than it should have been. I didn't want to sit next to him but wanted to sit down for a second while I figured out if I was going to leave.

I walked over to the lounge chair and sat. I sat down at the bottom and turned just in time to see Daren standing in the patio door, looking at me. He stood there for the longest time, just staring at me. I looked away. When I looked back, he was gone. I suddenly felt a chill go up my spine and knew that I had trouble coming my way. For a moment, I felt nauseous. I blinked several times, closed my eyes, and grabbed my stomach.

I let out a breath when I realized I had been holding it and put my head down into my hands. Suddenly I decided that I was ready to go.

"Derrick, can you drive Vicki home?"

I realized that Derrick was frowning at me. His hazel eyes were dark. He had that same darkness in his eyes that I had seen in his brother's. I frowned back and looked away. Sometimes I forgot that he and Daren were brothers. But in that moment, I was quickly reminded.

"Yeah, Maya, not a problem. I can take her home," he said as he looked away. It was at that moment when I realized that Derrick may be a problem as well. Letting out an agitated breath I stood.

"Don't leave yet, Maya. I really wanted to get to know you."

I turned and looked at Phillip. I forgot he was there. "Oh, sorry, Phillip. I really don't feel well, and I need to go home and get some rest."

"I will walk you to your car, pretty lady," he said, grabbing my arm into his. It took everything in me not to pull away.

"You don't have to do that, Phillip."

"I know I don't have to, Maya, but I want to."

We started toward the patio door, and I stopped to say bye to Mr. and Mrs. Clark, promising to return to see them soon and giving them my love. Mr. Clark made me a huge to-go plate and gave me a huge bear hug.

I felt out of sorts. I wished the day would start all over again so that I could do things much differently, make clearer decisions. I never would have allowed Daren and me to sleep together. I knew I shouldn't have let it happen.

"Are you okay?"

I jumped and sucked in a breath. "Shit! Oh, Phillip. Yes, yes. I'm fine. I just really need to get home."

"Will you be okay driving home, Maya?" He really looked concerned.

"Oh, yes, Phillip, thanks for asking." I put on another fake smile and nodded my head. I would try anything to hurry this up so that I could leave this foolishness.

I looked around for Daren as we walked through the house and toward the front door. There were no signs of him. But then I caught sight of him in the kitchen, hugged up with Kiera, and I stopped in my tracks. She noticed me and shot me the finger. He looked up and smirked as he leaned down to kiss her shoulder, his dark eyes sparkling with mischief.

"Um," I said, and I turned and continued walking toward the front door, where Phillip was waiting.

Once at my car, I turned and extended my hand. "It was nice meeting you, Phillip." He took my hand and smiled and shook it.

"Maya, you are very beautiful. I would love to get to know you. Are you spoken for?"

I let out a frustrated breath and scowled up at him.

"Phillip. Right now, I'm open for friendship. That's all I can offer. Is that okay with you?"

"Sure. Friendship would be great. Please give me a call," he said as he reached me a card.

I smiled as I took it and put it in my purse. "Sure. Enjoy the party," I said as I unlocked the car door and slid in and carefully placed my to-go plate of food on the passenger seat.

I sat there for a second to gather my racing thoughts. The things that happened in that house happened too fast. They happened so fast my head was spinning. My body was still tingling. I had to admit, I didn't expect his reaction afterward. I was looking forward to something new without the attachment of saying we were "girlfriend or boyfriend." I just wanted pleasure every now and then. I shook my head and leaned my forehead onto the steering wheel. I was hoping that I hadn't ruined my friendship with Daren. I had no intentions of hurting him. I just really needed some. It had been two years. And for one moment, I was very selfish. I should have said no, but I was weak. I really didn't know how I would fix our friendship, but I had to. I would wait on Vicki to sober up and get her to help me with this before it got too late to repair.

I jumped as I heard a loud knock on the window and banged my head on the steering wheel.

Putting the key into the ignition, I turned it to allow me to let the window down. It was Daren. There was something dark in those hazel eyes. It was a look of disgust and a look of hate. And it was aimed at me.

"Maya, we are cool. No worries. Kiera has been wanting a relationship with me for a long time. I don't have anything to lose, so I think I will give it a try. Don't worry about me. What happened in the restroom won't get out. Have a good evening, and be safe on your way home." With that, he turned and walked away.

I realized that my mouth was wide open and quickly closed it. Shaking my head, I started the car and pulled from the curb and down the street.

I didn't know how I got home, but I pulled my cousin's car into the driveway and got out and walked toward the front door.

Disarming the alarm with my remote and unlocking the front door, I walked in.

The cool air in the house hit me as I closed the door and locked it. I slid down to the cool tile floor and sat with my head against the door.

"What the hell just happened? Girl! Get it together. Daren was good, but he gave you what you wanted, and that was sex. Stop walking in that fog that you are in. Shit!" I spoke aloud in the quiet house.

I jumped up from the floor and headed for the kitchen. I reached up with the remote and armed the house and threw my keys in the basket on the table in the foyer as I walked past it.

Grabbing a bottle of wine and a wineglass, I headed upstairs to run a hot bubble bath in my tub.

Sitting on the side of the tub, I watched as the water ran, still deep in thought. I was naked and sipping on a glass of wine, relaxing. I slid down into the tub and smiled as I listened to the music that was playing. It was Kem. *I love me some Kem*, I thought as I leaned my head back against the tub pillow and hit the button to start the jets in the tub. Closing my eyes, I felt so relaxed.

I sat in that tub until the water was ice cold, bathed, and stepped out. I had finished the whole bottle of wine and began to stumble then giggle as I almost hit the floor. I slid into white boy shorts and a white T-shirt and some white socks and climbed into my bed. It was only 6:00 p.m., but that wine had me sleepy. Falling asleep quickly, I slept hard. I had strange dreams about Daren, where I kept seeing his face. Everywhere I went, he was there. He kept saying over and over, if he couldn't have me, then no one else would. I woke up screaming and flailing my arms.

I realized that I was just dreaming and began to focus my eyes. It was dark, and the clock read 11:17. The phone rang and further startled me.

"Shit!" I screamed, reaching for the phone.

"Hello?" I croaked. I could hear background noise, but whoever it was didn't say anything. Pulling the phone away from my face, I looked at the caller ID. It read, *Private Caller*. "Hello." This time, whoever it was hung up.

I hung the phone up. Wrapping my arms around me, I got a strange feeling but quickly shook it off.

I turned on the TV and turned off the music that was still playing. It wasn't long before I had drifted off to sleep again. No dreams this time.

CHAPTER 3

Party Planning

When I woke the next morning, I realized that I didn't set the alarm for church. It was 12:15 p.m. I had already missed service. I groaned as I rolled over. I didn't know what I was going to do for the day. I didn't have any plans, and I was surprised that Vicki hadn't called about her car.

The phone rang, and I reached over to answer. "Hello."

"What's up, cousin!" Vicki yelled.

"I don't understand you. You drink like crazy, and you still manage to wake up the next day very happy. What's your secret?"

"Oh, girl, I don't know. Maybe I'm all perky because my baby took care of me last night."

"Oh, you are at Derrick's house?"

"Yeah, girl, since you stole my car."

"I did not steal your car," I said as we both laughed.

"Vicki, you were too far gone to be talking about driving home. Besides, I had to get the hell out of there. I felt so uncomfortable."

"Why, girl, what happened? I introduced you to Phillip, and the next thing I know, you were gone. Oh! Derrick just mumbled something about you and Daren. Did something happen between you and him yesterday?"

"What! What did Derrick say? Girl, where are you? Come over, and I will make us some lunch and we can talk."

"I am still at Derrick's house. He just went to shower. When he gets out, I will have him drop me off."

We hung up, and I got up took a shower and made my way downstairs to figure out lunch.

An hour later, Vicki rang the doorbell then used her key and alarm remote to let herself in. Right behind her was Derrick. He averted his hazel eyes away from mine after frowning.

"Hello there to you two lovebirds."

"What's up, chick!" Vicki said as she gave me a big hug. Derrick gave me a weak hug, never meeting my eyes.

"I'm not staying. I just wanted to drop Vicki off and say hello. Daren and I are going to Mom and Dad's house to do some repairs on their fence."

When Derrick said his brother's name, he looked me in the eyes.

"Derrick, are you pissed at me for something?" I said and put my hand on my hip.

"No, why do you ask?"

"Well, yesterday at your parents' party, I know you saw the display between Daren and me. You had this look on your face, and I'm sure you were basing that off how your brother and I were looking at each other."

"Whatever you and my brother have going on is between you two," he said in a huff.

"I understand that, Derrick, but your whole attitude toward me has changed, and I thought you and I were close. But I understand very well that blood is thicker than water."

"Yes, it is, but you are right. I did get a funny vibe from you two when I saw my brother at the patio door. So naturally, I assumed the look on his face had something to do with you. Look, Maya. You know my brother has been in love with you since he first laid eyes on you. Please don't hurt him. He wears his heart on his shoulder, and he has been through a lot."

"Derrick, like I told your brother, and now I will tell you. I don't want a relationship with him other than friendship, but your brother keeps pushing the issue. I am not in the business of intentionally hurting people. Now, he and I did have a little misunderstanding, but I promise I will get with him and repair our friendship."

His face softened, and he finally met my eyes.

Derrick leaned down and gave me a hug. "Okay, Maya. We have always been cool. I apologize for the attitude."

"You are forgiven, Derrick." I punched him in the arm, and we both smiled.

Vicki was standing with a smirk on her face and was very quiet. I had forgotten that she was standing there.

"Mm-hm, y'all don't need to have any misunderstandings. You two are like sister and brother. Don't let that shit happen again." We all laughed.

Vicki hugged and kissed Derrick, and I turned to walk into the kitchen while they were saying their goodbyes.

I heard the door chime as it opened and closed, and I heard Vicki walking toward the kitchen.

"Girl! What was that about?"

I had our lunch set up at the bar and was placing the napkins next to the plates. Motioning for my cousin to have a seat, I sat as well.

"Vicki, yesterday at the party, Daren was following me around like a little lost puppy. I finally got the drop on him after telling him that I wanted to speak to his dad without an escort. I ate my food outside then made my way back into the house. Girl, I fell asleep in the TV room with some old ladies, and when I woke up, Daren was all on me."

"What do you mean all on you? That sounds freaky." We laughed.

"Vicki! Listen. So when I got up to leave, Daren asked me if he could kiss me."

"Shut up! About time he made some kind of a damn move."

"Whatever that means, girl. Anyway, he was telling me what he wanted to do to me. It got a little hot in the room. Before I knew it, he had backed me up against the wall and kissed me. And, Vicki, he made me wet just with that kiss. Well, to make a long story short, we ended up having sex in the restroom."

"What! How was it! If he is anything like his brother, then I know he is packing and good at what he does. I need more details than that. How did you get to the point where you are having sex in the restroom?"

"I walked in there to get myself together from that kiss. And then he walked in there on me. He told me that he understood that I didn't want a relationship but thought that we could hook up from time to time. I was cool with that. He kissed me, saying he wanted to leave me with something to think about. Next thing I know, he has me in the air on his shoulders, and he was licking on me like it was his last meal. Then we were on the toilet, then on the floor. My body tingled all night, and this morning, when I woke up, it was still tingling."

"So when did it all go south?"

"Afterward he said that he didn't think he could just sleep with me and be okay with it. So I got up cleaned myself off and went outside looking for you. After Phillip walked me to your car, Daren came outside told me not to worry about it, we were cool. He also said that he decided to start a relationship with Kiera."

"Are you serious? Bad move. That broad is nutty. Aww, poor Daren. My cousin whipped it on him and made him fall too deep."

"Girl, whatever. I feel bad. I saw all kinds of red flags, but I hadn't had any in two years, Vicki. He offered, and my body answered for me. It was so good, girl!"

We sat and laughed until we were red in the face. But in the back of my mind, I wanted to know if he was okay and decided that I would call him later and patch up our friendship.

"Well, I got so drunk at Mr. and Mrs. Jackson's party that I passed out on the chair out by the pool. Derrick had to carry me to his car. When I woke up this morning, it took me a minute to try and figure out where I was."

"Your ass needs to slow down on all that drinking and maybe go to a damn AA meeting."

"Yeah, cousin, don't I know it. Oh yeah, before I forget. What did you think about Phillip?"

"Oh, he was nice."

"That's it, Maya, he was nice?"

"I mean, what else can I say? I was only there about five minutes after meeting him, and then I left."

"Ooh! I have an idea, Maya. Don't say no!"

"Oh no! Oh, hell no, Vicki! The answer is no, whatever it is! Whenever you get like this, it's never good."

"Cousin, hear me out. You will love this idea! Why don't you throw a dinner party? We can invite a few guests. It can be couples. And you can invite Phillip. What do you think?"

"Hmm, that's the best idea you have ever had. Sure, if you help me put it together." I smiled, thinking about that exciting idea.

"Girl, I got you. Let's throw it next weekend."

"Um, okay. Who should we invite?"

"I really think we should invite Daren and his new girlfriend, Kiera. Maybe she will stop being such a bitch if she gets to know you on your own turf."

"Vicki, I don't know if I want that crazy broad in my house."

"Don't worry, cousin. I will have a little talk with her."

"Well, okay. As long as she does not come in my house with her usual drama, they are invited."

By the time we had completed the list, it came to a total of five couples: Kiera and Daren, Vicki and Derrick, Phillip and I. We contacted Phillip to extend the invitation, and he added his two brothers and their girls: Max and his girl, Cynthia, and Dominic and his girl, Tandy.

I got up to clear the dishes and get my kitchen back in order, and my cousin decided to leave and get some rest for work the next day. It was going on 4:00 p.m., and I wanted to get some more rest to get myself ready for the next day.

The doorbell rang, jarring me out of my thoughts, and I almost dropped a plate. I tipped over to the window to look out onto the street and in the driveway for a familiar car. I didn't like opening my door if I wasn't expecting anyone. The doorbell chimed again. Sitting in my driveway was Daren's car. I groaned and debated on answering the door and quickly decided that he and I did need to talk.

Opening the door, I greeted him with a smile that was not returned.

"We need to talk," he said as he brushed past me into my foyer.

"Sure, I was going to call you anyway. We can go into the den and talk in there."

I quickly chose a chair to keep my distance between Daren and me so that he wouldn't get any ideas.

He stood uncomfortably in front of the couch then walked over to the other chair and plopped down hard in it, letting out a burst of air.

"Maya, I really value our friendship, and I wanted to apologize for how I behaved. I really do hope you forgive me."

I exhaled the breath that I was holding. "Daren, I'm glad that you came by because I was going to call you anyway. We have known each other way too long to let something like this tarnish our relationship. Of course, I forgive you. Please forgive me for my part in this. I should not have allowed this to happen."

He smiled, and I felt relief.

"Oh, before I forget, I want to invite you and Kiera to my couples' dinner party next Saturday if you two don't have any plans."

The smile quickly left his face, and his hazel eyes grew dark. He frowned then closed his eyes and put his head down into his hands.

"No, we don't have any plans. We will be here."

"What's wrong?"

"What do you mean?"

"Why did you frown after I extended the invitation? You don't seem happy. Talk to me. We are friends, and I'm here if you need me."

"I know how you feel about Kiera. She is a handful, and I just don't want her to come in here, causing any problems. I will make sure that I speak with her."

"Yes, because all I'm trying to do is extend the olive branch. I don't have time for the drama, and if she brings any, she will be put out of my house."

"No worries, Maya. I will talk to her. So what are you up to today?"

"Nothing. Vicki came by earlier with Derrick. He said you and he had to go fix your parents' fence."

"Yeah, don't worry. I didn't tell him anything."

"Shut the hell up, Daren. Y'all are brothers. I know you told him everything. Just don't tell anyone else."

We laughed and sat there and talked for about an hour. It felt good to have my friend back.

His cell phone rang, cutting our conversation. Pulling it out of his pocket and glancing at the caller ID, he groaned. "Kiera, what's up?"

He sat there quietly, and I could hear her loud mouth over the phone. "I'm on my way. Bye."

He let out an angry breath and finally made eye contact with me. His eyes were dark. So much anger, and it felt like it was at me. He quickly shook it off.

"Daren, are you okay?"

"Maya, I'm going to ask you something. This will be the last that we speak of this, and I won't bring it up again. Is that okay with you?"

"Um, okay. Sure. Go for it. Say what you have to say. But if it is what I think it is, please don't bring it up anymore once you leave today."

"Do you think that you will ever love me like I love you?"

"No, Daren. Honestly, no."

"So me making love to you yesterday meant nothing to you?"

"That shit is funny, Daren. Men are a trip. Sex is only that, sex. Sex is what you and I had, nothing more and nothing less than that. Making love is for couples in love. You have been family to me since I can remember. Yes, I gave in to my weakness and had sex with you. It shouldn't have happened. So many alarms went off in my head, but I ignored them. I was weak for the sex. I was hoping that we could just help each other out from time to time because, my friend, you put it down. But I see you put your feelings in it, and I know that it can't happen again. I'm sorry for being so blunt. Hopefully, we can let this go."

We sat in silence. I was staring at him, and he was staring at the floor.

He slowly stood. "Thanks for your honesty, Maya. No hard feelings. I'm going to focus on this relationship with Kiera."

"Daren, don't you think that it's unfair to her? How can you go in a relationship with someone when you have feelings for someone else? All you are going to do is hurt her in the long run."

He finally met my eyes. I saw sadness in his eyes. He was my friend, and I didn't want him to hurt. I wanted him happy. But I wanted him to get past his feelings for me before he went half-assed into a relationship. I wouldn't wish heartbreak on my worst enemy. It took me two years to heal, and I knew how it felt to love someone with everything in me and not have it returned.

"I just wish you could feel what I feel for you, Maya." He reached up and touched my face and pushed hair away from my eye.

He leaned down and placed a lingering kiss on my lips. My body started tingling again, and I took in a breath. He broke that kiss then turned and walked toward the door.

"What about Kiera, Daren? Don't you care about her feelings? Don't you want to make sure that you don't hurt her?"

"As time passes, Maya, I will feel more for her. For now, it feels good having someone show so much interest in me. It makes me feel wanted. Maybe one day I can love her. All I know is, I will never love anyone like I love you. Hey, Maya, I remember you used to be a little softer than you are now. I see pain in your eyes. You stay to yourself, and I never hear about you dating anyone. You haven't been with anyone since you and Miles, and it has been two years. What happened?"

Hearing that name brought chills to me, and I closed my eyes tight, hoping to shake that feeling. I felt bile rise up in my throat. Swallowing, I opened then closed my eyes again. Opening them, I frowned as I made eye contact with Daren. I shook my head as if to say that I didn't want to talk about it.

"Maya, we used to be close. We were really close. All that stopped when you started dating Miles." He lightly touched my arm, and I jumped.

"Yes, because you always had something bad to say about Miles. I was in love and got tired of you bad-mouthing him," I said through clenched teeth. He flinched, and I let out a breath and softened my face.

"But, Maya, I wasn't lying about anything that I said to you about him. Miles was and still is a dog. He wasn't good enough for you. What happened? It's good to talk about what's bothering us. It really helps to get past things."

"Daren, I'm healed, and I'm so past Miles. He hurt me, broke my heart. There is nothing else to say about it."

"Come and sit down next to me and tell me about it, my friend." Daren grabbed my hand and led me to the couch. I sat and so did he.

He patted me on the knee. "Go ahead, I'm listening."

"I thought you were going to meet with Kiera?"

"I was, Maya, but this is important."

I knew Daren was right. I told my cousin that Miles cheated on me, but I didn't give her the whole story.

Exhaling, I prepared to tell him my deepest, darkest secrets. I was getting ready to relive a lot of pain and needed that extra breath to help me along.

CHAPTER 4

A Part of You and I

I sat Indian style on the sofa, and I glanced at Daren. He patted my leg as if to say, go ahead, and that he was listening.

Suddenly, I didn't feel as strong as I had been. I felt sad. So much pain started rushing up into me, and I buried my head into my hands and stifled a scream. I could feel Daren rubbing on my back. I thought I had gotten past this, but the pain that I felt seemed as if the hurt happened just yesterday.

"I'm here, my friend. Let it out. You will feel better. Let it all out, Maya."

Wiping the tears from my eyes, I took a deep breath and began.

"Daren, Miles was my everything and then some. I loved him more than I have ever loved anyone. I gave him all of me. He made me feel beautiful. We spent every waking moment together. I loved him body, heart, and soul. I would have given my life for him. I felt secure. I felt loved. For a year, we could not be separated. We decided to move in together and started renting a house in Spring, Texas. Six more months passed, and I woke up one morning, very sick. My cycles came like clockwork, so I knew for a week that I might be pregnant. Miles got up and left for work, and I called and made a doctor's appointment. I didn't want to tell him until it was confirmed." My words were slow and deliberate. I was trying to shorten the story, but it was if it hurt me to speak it.

"Maya, you had a baby?"

"Let me finish, Daren. Please."

"Okay, I'm sorry."

"My appointment was confirmed for noon. I got up and got myself dressed. I was so sick that day and was eating crackers and drinking ginger ale, trying to settle my stomach. I was excited but scared because Miles and I never talked about a future together. Never talked about marriage, and we never talked about having kids together. I wasn't sure how he would take the situation." I looked over at Daren, and his mouth was open. "Daren..."

"Don't worry about me, Maya. I'm just so surprised that you never told me. Well, I understand that we weren't close anymore, and for that, I am sorry. I should have been there for you."

I exhaled and decided not to reply but to continue with my story. I wanted to hurry and get it out of my mouth.

"The doctor confirmed it. I was six weeks pregnant. Everything he said after that news was a blur. I was scared, and I didn't know how I would tell Miles that we were getting ready to have a baby. I rushed home and decided that I would tell him over dinner. I made dinner, set the table, and got myself ready for the evening. I was so exhausted and decided to take a nap for an hour."

I felt Daren's hand on my shoulder. "Maya, you are shaking. Are you sure that you want to continue with this?"

"Yeah, I need to get this off my chest."

"Okay, Maya, take your time."

He grabbed my hand and gave it a squeeze. That gave me the strength that I needed, and I managed a weak smile as I met his eyes.

"I took a shower after my nap and put on a cute dress. I put my hair up and sprayed on the perfume he loved to smell on me. When he walked in and saw me, he smiled. He gave me a big hug and a kiss. We had a lovely evening. It was very romantic. After we ate, we went into the living room and sat and talked and laughed. I felt that it was time, and I told him that I had something to tell him. I just blurted it out. I was smiling, happy because we had made something so beautiful, and it was growing inside me. He didn't react like I thought he would. My heart dropped to the pit of my stomach. He got up and walked toward the bedroom, and I got up and followed him. I asked him what he thought. He told me that he didn't want any kids right then. Had other things he wanted to do before he became someone's dad. I was so hurt. I was devastated."

"Oh, Maya, I'm so sorry. What happened after that?"

"Well, for a few weeks, we just existed in the house together. He didn't have but a few words to say to me each day. Finally, over dinner, he told me that we couldn't be together if I decided to keep the baby. I was hurt, shook my head okay, and do you know what I did, Daren?"

"What?"

"The next day, when Miles went to work, I got up and packed my stuff and started making plans to move out. There was no way that I was giving up something so beautiful. But in my frantic attempt to hurry and get my stuff moved, I fell down the front steps, landing on my stomach and on my head. The neighbor found me and called the ambulance."

"Oh no, Maya!"

I glanced over at him as he put his hand on my thigh. I was crying and trying to catch my breath. Daren pulled me to him and held me until I collected myself enough to tell him the rest.

Sitting back up and wiping my face, I began again.

"When I woke up in the hospital, Miles was there, asleep in the chair next to the bed. I just laid there and stared at him. I still had so much love for him, and I prayed that he would finally accept our baby. The doctor came in the room, and Miles woke up. He grabbed my hand when he saw that I was awake, and we both were waiting to hear what the doctor had to say. And he said it. And it was like my world had ended. There was no more fetus. He called my baby a fetus. The fall was too much for that tiny life. The child that I was so excited about was gone, was no more. I cried. For days, I cried. I wouldn't get out of the bed. Before I knew it, months had passed. I finally found the strength to get myself together. I had lost a lot of weight. I realized that somewhere along the way, Miles had started spending his time elsewhere. About a week later, Miles moved out. Told me that he was moving in with a woman that was having his baby. She was five months pregnant. He wanted a life with her. He said he was sorry and left."

"Wow, Maya. I am so sorry. I knew he was with someone else. They never hid it. He didn't care. He was with you and her."

"Love blinds you, Daren. It does." I stood. "Give me a sec. I want to wipe my face. I will be right back."

When I came back into the room, Daren was sitting, looking at a photo album that I kept on the shelf.

He stood when I came into the room and put the album back on the shelf.

"Are you okay?"

"Oh yes. Like I said, I'm over Miles. I cry for my child. I never got to see or hold him or her. After all that happened, I put all my focus on my career. I moved out of that house after I had this one built. Now here I am. I'm stronger, Daren. And I'm wiser. I know my worth and will not settle. But for right now, I don't want a relationship. I hope that you understand."

"I do. I'm sorry for pushing the issue. I'm truly sorry. I felt that if we slept together that maybe your eyes would open, and you would feel for me what I feel for you. I understand now, and I'm content with just being your friend."

We hugged, and he left after taking another call from Kiera. He was frowning. I hoped that she didn't run him ragged. I hoped that she didn't hurt him.

I smiled. I was happy to have my friend back. I knew time would make us closer like we were.

CHAPTER 5

How Sweet

That Monday was a blur. I was very busy at work, and before I knew it, it was 7:30 p.m., and I realized that other than the cleaning people, I was the only one in my department still at work. I sat back in my chair and turned it so that I could look out my window. I needed to give my eyes a break. My eyes snapped open, and I had a thought to call Phillip. He tried to call me the night before, and I decided not to answer. I remembered that he had left a message and turned around to pick up my cell phone.

Putting it on speaker, I accessed my voicemail.

This deep voice came through and made me close my eyes, sent chills down my spine, and made me squeeze my legs together tightly. "Maya, I just wanted to hear your voice and tell you good night. When you have a moment, give me a call. Good night and pleasant dreams, beautiful."

I listened to that message two more times before I got the nerve to call back.

He answered on the third ring. "Hello."

"Phillip?" I said, shocked that he answered.

"Yes?"

"Hi, this is Maya. Returning your call. How are you?" I was stumbling over my words because I was so nervous.

"Maya, it is really good to hear your voice, beautiful. How are you? How was your day?"

I smiled at his concern and paused to get my words together before I answered. "Thanks, Phillip. I am well, thank you for asking, and my day is still going on."

"What do you mean?"

I giggled like a schoolgirl and found myself swinging back and forth in my chair. "I'm still at work."

"Oh, Maya, is that normal for you to work so late?" He had so much concern in his voice.

"Well, yes. I am very dedicated to my job. It keeps me busy." I laughed.

He laughed an easy laugh. "What's funny, Ms. Workaholic?"

"I sounded like a commercial. I just thought it was funny. Anyway, Phillip, how was your day?"

He laughed. "No, you didn't sound like a commercial. It just sounded like you have to explain that a lot. And to answer your question, I had a good day. You calling me made it a wonderful day. It really is good to hear your voice. Hey, Maya, why don't you let me take you to dinner tonight? Let me get you away from that office?"

"Mmmm, I don't know. I really do have a heavy workload." I was stalling. I really wanted to have dinner with him, but didn't want to seem so eager. I wasn't desperate and didn't want to agree so quickly and make him think that I was easy. I was not easy.

"I understand. But you do need to eat. Where do you work? I could pick you up and drop you back off. Or I could pick up something and come to your job, and we could eat there."

"Well, you coming here would give me a chance to work a little more. That sounds like a good idea."

I quickly gave him directions to my job and hung up. I was smiling. I didn't know what it was about this man, but he really had me interested. I walked to the restroom and touched up my makeup and fluffed my naturally curly, shoulder-length hair. I added some gloss to my lips and walked to the elevators to meet him downstairs. He arrived twenty minutes later, and I hit the red button to let him in.

He had two white plastic bags and a big brown bag. I held the glass door open for him to pass through. When he walked past me, the aroma from the bag hit me, and my stomach began to growl. I closed the door and made sure that it was secure. I paused and closed my eyes then opened them before turning around. I had to get myself ready to really see what had just walked through the door.

Slowly turning, I took in all of him: tall, beautiful smile, and skin the color of sweet dark chocolate. He smiled and walked toward me. He had placed the bags on the chair in the lobby and headed my way as if he was on a mission, and I was his mission. I prepared myself for what I knew he was about to do.

"Hi, beautiful," he said as he stood in front of me.

His sexy, deep voice vibrated through my body. I had to look up to meet his eyes. His teeth were so white. I took in his smells. I picked up the smell of mint on his breath, the fresh scent of soap, and cologne. He was freshly shaven, hair freshly cut, beautiful, clear skin. Everything seemed in place with his body. Very attractive man. Damn that this brother was fine. I was anxious to have a conversation with him, find out more about him. I smirked.

"Hi, handsome." I decided to flirt a little. What could it hurt?

He smiled and grabbed my arms, which were wrapped around my body and pulled me into him. I dropped my arms to my side and started to panic. It was way too soon for a kiss. *Please don't kiss me*, I screamed in my head. With one hand, he reached up and pushed my hair from my face. He kissed my forehead, then my cheek. Then he wrapped his arms around my shoulders and hugged me. I wrapped my arms around his waist and leaned into him. I closed my eyes and inhaled his scent.

He moaned, kissed the top of my head, and released me. "Are you hungry?"

"Yes," I croaked then cleared my throat.

He turned and walked over to the bags and picked them up.

"Can I help you with anything, Phillip?"

"No, just lead the way." He smiled.

I turned and headed to the elevator. I glanced back over my shoulder and thought I saw a familiar figure standing in front of the door, and I stopped. The figure turned and quickly walked past the door. Something was so familiar about that dark figure. The walk was familiar. I just couldn't figure it out. I caught a chill and quickly shook it off and turned to catch up with Phillip.

We stepped in together, and I pushed the button to my floor, and the doors closed. Turning in his direction, I took a long look at him. He was gazing at me, smiling, and I smiled, feeling my face turn hot. I knew that I was blushing, and my eyes widened, and I looked down at my feet.

"Did you have a hard time finding the building?" I asked, looking back at his face.

"No. It's funny that we hadn't met before. I work in the next building." He chuckled. "But then again, you rarely leave your desk, right, Ms. Workaholic?"

I laughed. "Right."

We fell silent but continued to stare at each other. I broke the gaze, blinking hard once again. I looked down at my feet. There definitely was some attraction between us. There was no denying that.

The elevator finally arrived, and we stepped off. I badged us in, and I turned and led him to my office. Once inside, I closed the door and turned the light on over the round table in my office. The lamp wasn't very bright and offered the ambiance that was perfect for this impromptu dinner.

"Please have a seat, beautiful. Let me cater to you."

I giggled out of pure nervousness and did what he asked.

I turned and sat. He wanted to cater to me. *Wow. It's going to take more than you bringing me dinner and setting it up to get in my pants, buddy. You are going to have to wait,* I thought as I sat, smiling.

From one bag, he brought out two white cloths that looked like they contained something. He smiled at me as he unwrapped them. They were long-stemmed wine flutes.

"Wow. Fancy," I said, and we both laughed.

"I have nothing but the finest Boone's Farm for such a beautiful lady." We met eyes and both fell out laughing.

"Boone's Farm, huh? Wow, I'm impressed you went all out for this occasion."

"No, Maya, I'm only joking," he said as he took a wine box out and pulled out a bottle of white wine. I smiled but said nothing.

He opened the brown bag and took out two containers. The aroma was strong, and my stomach began to growl. When he sat a container in front of me, I realized that it was from Boudreaux's Cajun Kitchen. I frowned and leaned closer as he took the top off.

"Who told you that this was my favorite? I love the Pasta Lafayette from Boudreaux's." I sat back in my chair and put my arms in my lap. "You must have been talking to Vicki or Derrick." I laughed.

"Well, I wasn't sure what you liked and didn't want to call you back, so I called Derrick. Of course, he and your cousin were together, and she told me what you like. Hey, you can't blame me for wanting to please you," he said, holding his hands out, palms up.

"No, you get a lot of points for this, Mr. Phillip." I gave him a thumbs-up with one hand.

He sat down. "Well, I have dessert also, pretty lady. So make sure you save room." He winked, and I smiled.

"Well, sir. I have a huge appetite, and I can promise you that even after eating this garlic bread, pasta, and drinking this wine, I will have more than enough room for dessert."

He laughed a deep laugh, leaned back, and closed his eyes. "For such a very tiny woman, you are telling me that you can put away some food?"

"Yes. I work out, believe it or not. I work a lot, but I make sure that I get up every morning and get it in. That is the only way that I can continue to eat like a piggy."

We bowed our heads, and he said a short prayer over the food, and we both said, "Amen."

It was quiet for the first ten minutes while we both ate. We stole glances at each other and smiled. I was starving, so filling my stomach a little was all that was on my mind.

He wiped his mouth and sipped his wine. His eyes were on me again as he sat back in his chair. No smile. I couldn't read him. I felt uncomfortable. His stare was intense. "Tell me about you. I want to know everything," he said, almost in a whisper.

I cleared my throat, wiped my mouth, then sat back in my chair. I studied him for a second. "Um, okay. I'm thirty-five. I have a bachelor's in finance. I'm working on starting my own business. My family is from Louisiana. I live in the same neighborhood as my mom and stepfather. I'm single, no children. I own my own house. I can't think of anything else to tell you. I really don't go out much. Lately, Vicki has been dragging me to strange parties. Other than that, I try and get to church as often as possible."

He never moved and never broke his stare. I couldn't read the look on his face. I put my fork down. I didn't realize that I was still holding it. I looked away and grabbed my wineglass and took a few sips then wiped my mouth with my napkin.

"I hate to sound so cliché, but why are you single? You are absolutely beautiful. And before you say it, yes, I know that beauty has nothing to do with your status. But, wow. Maya, you are breathtaking, smart, and you are obviously doing well for yourself. But you have a sadness in your eyes that comes and goes. Just as quickly as it comes, it's gone, and it's replaced with a little hardness. You throw this wall up, and it's hard to get through."

I had begun eating again. I couldn't look at him. He was reading me like a book. I wasn't sure if I was ready for such a deep conversation my first time hanging with him. I was frowning, and I could feel myself getting angry.

I stopped and let my fork drop. I could feel myself growing very angry and wanted to tell him to leave. I looked up at him, and his eyes were wide.

"Maya, I didn't mean any harm. It's just something about you. Since I first met you, I just felt as if I needed to take care of you." He leaned back and put his head in his hands. "Damn it. I'm sorry, Maya. I hope I haven't offended you. If I have, I do apologize."

I softened and leaned back in my chair. I was working on not putting everyone in that same basket. The asshole basket was what I called it. "Um, it's my turn to apologize, Phillip. I am a very guarded person. I've been hurt so bad by the ones whom I thought loved me. So I have a wall up. I don't mean to come off so hard. I like you. There is something about you, some kind of pull, and I don't understand it. I feel as if I've known you for a long time, like our paths have crossed before, and I've never met you. I, however, don't want you to feel as if you need to take care of me. That is very sweet, but I can take care of myself." I decided to smile to break the tension that was so thick in the room.

His body appeared to relax, and he smiled and nodded his head. "I understand where you are coming from, but I want you to understand that I am a very blunt person. I tend to say what's on my mind. Not to the point where it's obnoxious. I just like to speak my mind."

"It's fine, Phillip. I'm the same way. As long as you are honest with me while we are getting to know each other, we shouldn't have any problems."

Phillip rose and started clearing the food containers and laid out smaller containers with pecan pie. I smiled.

When he sat down, he looked at me and smiled. "Yes, your cousin told me you love pecan pie also."

We laughed together, and it felt good. We ate again in silence, and I decided to drill him.

"So, Phillip, tell me about you. What makes you tick?"

He smiled. "Well, pretty lady, I am thirty-eight years old. I also have a bachelor's degree in finance, and I have my CPA. I am a controller. I own my own home. My parents live twenty minutes from me. I'm single, no kids. I work a lot, but I manage to hang out with my friends from time to time. I'm a homebody. I would rather read a good book or watch a movie than hang out in a club. There is nothing but trouble in a club. I try and get to church as often as possible." He smiled.

"Okay, well, Phillip, let me sound cliché. You are a very handsome man. Why are you single?"

I saw something in his eyes. He looked past me for a second, focusing his eyes behind me. Then he looked back at me. His smile no longer spread from his eyes and down to his mouth. His eyes no longer smiled, only his mouth. So, to me, there was some pain. Someone had hurt him to his core like I had been hurt.

"I was in a relationship, actually engaged. About sixteen months ago, she decided that she didn't want to be tied down anymore. We lived together and had been together for four years by that time. She never really told me that until I found out that she had been sleeping with one of my boys. When I came home and he was there, I questioned her. He left quickly. She told me that they had been doing their own thing for a few months. Told me that all I did was work. Said she wanted to be free and single. And the next day, she packed up and left me while I was at work." He cleared his throat and smiled a weak smile.

"I'm sorry, Phillip. I can see the pain in your eyes."

I looked over at the sofa and asked if he wanted to sit on the sofa with me. We walked over and sat at the same time. I kicked my shoes off and tucked one foot underneath me and angled my body toward his.

"So, Phillip, are you healed? Have you forgiven her, and can you say that you have you moved on?"

I was comfortable with my arm on the back of the sofa and my head in the cup of my hand. I wanted him to feel comfortable enough to really open up to me. I wanted to hear his story. I wanted to hear about the pain that he wore on his face and the far-off look that he got when I asked him about it.

He smiled and touched my arm. "Yes," he whispered as he ran his hand down my arm.

I felt chills, and I pulled my arm away. *Too comfortable*, I thought and squinted my eyes at him.

He cleared his throat and smiled. "So tell me about the pain in your eyes, beautiful."

"Well, my relationship ended two years ago. To sum the whole story up, Phillip, we met and fell in love. We jumped right into moving in with each other. I got pregnant. He no longer wanted me and let me know that he didn't want the baby. Said he wasn't ready. I decided to move out. In the process of me moving out, I fell and lost the baby. After that, I fell into a deep depression. When he should have been by my side, he was with another woman. A woman who he was apparently seeing while he was seeing me and who was already pregnant with their baby. He moved out. End of relationship."

"Have you moved on, Maya? Have you healed?"

"Yes. I think about the time that I put in that relationship. There were so many red flags, and I chose to ignore them. I'm all about flags now. I'm all about protecting my heart, protecting myself from being hurt like that again."

We sat in silence. He was looking out the window, hand under his chin. He appeared to be in deep thought. I stared at his face, the frown he had. I wondered what he was thinking. I glanced at the clock. It was 11:15 p.m. I turned and looked at his face. He was looking at me. No smile this time. Again, I couldn't read him.

The silence in the room was deafening. I began to get uncomfortable and started fidgeting.

I cleared my throat. "It's getting late, Phillip."

"Yes, let me clean all this up and get you to your car."

We worked together in silence. Our conversation was still floating in the air. Neither one of us knew what to say, and neither one of us wanted to look at the other. It took us only a few minutes to clean up.

I powered down my computer and grabbed my purse and bag. We walked side by side to the elevators and stood close. He put his arm around me, and I looked up at his face, and he smiled. It was as if he was saying that everything would be okay. I felt safe, comfortable, and very much at ease. I smiled and put my arm around his waist and laid my head on his shoulder. We squeezed each other at the same time, and he kissed my forehead. So much closeness between us, and we hadn't known each other that long. But it seemed like we had known each other forever.

When the elevator dinged and opened, we separated, and I stepped out first. This time, he grabbed my hand. I noticed that he was a very affectionate person, and I liked that. This was new. The affection was new for me. But I knew I needed to keep things at a slow pace. Friendship was what I wanted, and we could build from that.

He walked me to my car and helped me get my things in, then he leaned over and fastened my seat belt. That act alone made me feel like letting down my guard with him.

"Get in, Phillip. I will drive you to the visitors' parking." He walked over, opened the door, and got in. Once he fastened his seat belt, I started the car and drove to the visitors' parking around the front of the building. I parked next to the only vehicle in the lot.

Phillip unbuckled his seat belt but just sat there. "Maya, I enjoyed our evening. I would love to see you again tomorrow if that's okay. I can take you out this time or whatever you want. But I really want to be near you." He was looking at his hands but looked in my eyes when he said that he wanted to be near me.

I realized that I wasn't breathing and took a breath.

"I would love that."

He smiled, but it quickly went away. He was staring at my lips, and I was staring at his. "I won't ask for a kiss because I know it's too soon. But, Maya, I'm fighting with myself here not to just steal a kiss. It's so against the man that I am. I am a perfect gentleman. So to keep me from getting slapped or taking something that I have not earned, I will get out of your car now."

I grabbed his face with both hands. I didn't know what I was doing. Something came over me. I pulled him toward me. He grabbed my hands and pulled me the rest of the way. Our lips touched, and both of us exhaled. He put one hand behind my head, and we both tilted our heads. My lips parted and let his tongue in. I sucked on it gently, then harder as the kiss deepened. He took his tongue from me, and I almost panicked. I didn't want that kiss to end. But instead of pulling away, he sucked on my bottom lip then my top. When our lips met again, I gave him my tongue. He sucked gently, and he moaned. We pulled back and gave tiny kisses to each other. He kissed my cheek and down to my neck and inhaled. Putting his arms around me, he gave me a big, awkward hug, and I squeezed him back.

"Good night, beautiful," he said as he moved hair from in front of my eye.

He leaned in, and we began our kiss again. The sucking and the moaning from both of us were the only sounds. The soft music that was playing was drowned out. I could feel my body heating up, and this time, I pulled back.

"Good night, handsome," I said in a shaky voice.

Phillip kissed my cheek again and planted tiny kisses on my lips again. I watched until he got in his car and closed it and buckled his seat belt.

I rode home in deep thought. When I pulled into my driveway and then my garage, I was still in deep thought as I watched the garage go down. It was late, but my body was still alive. I still felt Phillip's lips on mine, and I reached up and touched them. I quickly got out of the car and disarmed the house so that I could walk into the door.

The house was so dark. The only light I could see was from the light over the stove. I walked that way as I hit the button on the remote to arm the house. Turning on the light in the kitchen, I went straight to the fridge for a bottle of water. My cell phone rang, and the bottle dropped to the floor before I could open it. I grabbed my chest and dug in my pocket for my cell. It was him. I smiled.

"Hello."

"Hi. I just wanted to make sure you made it home safely."

"Oh yes, I made it home. Thanks for checking on me. That means a lot."

"Okay, well, get some rest. I'm looking forward to seeing you tomorrow."

"Did you make it home safely, Phillip?" I asked, trying to keep him on the phone. I leaned down and picked up the bottle of water, turned off the kitchen light, and headed for the stairs. Once in my room, I turned on the lamp next to the bed.

"Yes, I made it home. Thank you for asking, beautiful. You know, I miss you already." The last part he said in a whisper.

"Wow." I struggled to respond. I didn't want to seem too eager or to fast or whatever. I was scared. I was so scared at this point, and I frowned. I didn't want to rush into false emotion. Falling in lust was not something that I wanted to do. I decided not to say anything else.

"I don't expect you to respond to that, Maya. Sleep well."

"You do the same, Phillip. Good night." I held the phone, waiting for him to hang up. I think he was waiting for me to hang up.

"Hello?"

"I'm still here."

"Maya, I don't want to hang up. But it's getting late, and both of us have to get up. Why don't you shower and get settled for bed and call me back. I want to talk to you until you go to sleep."

I smiled. I felt like a teenager. My heart was beating fast. "Okay. I will call you once I get settled."

"Okay, talk to you in a few."

This time, I did hang up. I hurried and got my clothes laid out for my workout in the morning. I also laid out my clothes for work. I had no time for a long, hot bath, so I opted for a shower instead. The water was warm, and I wanted to stand there in that warmth to relax. I quickly soaped my body and washed my face. Once I rinsed the soap off, I turned on the cold water to cool my body down. I put on my normal outfit for bed: a white T-shirt, some white boy shorts, and a pair of white socks.

I climbed into my big, king-sized bed and reached over and turned off the lamp. I said my prayers then reached over for the house phone. I decided to call him from there.

He answered on the first ring but sounded out of breath.

"Hello."

"Hi."

"Did you enjoy your bath?"

I laughed. "I took a shower."

He laughed as well. "So did I. I was trying to hurry. I couldn't wait to talk with you."

I knew I was blushing. "Same here, Phillip."

"Whenever you get sleepy, let me know, or just go ahead and go to sleep. No need to hang up. It will make me feel as if I'm holding you as you sleep."

"Okay," I said almost in a whisper.

"I'm glad you let me spend some time with you today. I felt like a schoolboy." He chuckled.

"Yes, it was good to see you too. And you have made me feel like a teenager since I first spoke with you."

My eyes were getting heavy, and I didn't want to be rude and fall asleep on him even though he said it was okay. "Phillip," I whispered.

"Mmmm, yes, baby," he whispered back.
"I'm sleepy." I laughed.
"Okay. Get some rest. Good night, beautiful."
"Good night, handsome."

CHAPTER 6

Hanging Out

I hit the snooze button so many times the next morning. I wasn't able to work out. I dragged myself out of bed and got in the shower. I would definitely need a cup of coffee or two this morning. I quickly co-washed my hair with coconut conditioner and my body with coconut body scrub and got out of the shower. With my towel wrapped around me, I walked to the mirror and applied olive oil and butter cream to my hair. I took six different sections and twisted my naturally curly hair up and pinned it up until I could get dressed, and then I would untwist it and apply a little eco-styler gel to hold my curls.

I grabbed yogurt, a container of fresh fruit, a stick of string cheese, a premade salad with turkey and lemons on the side, and a pack of hummus for lunch, and a granola bar in case I wanted something sweet. I put all my food in my lunch bag, grabbed my purse, keys, and cell phone, and headed for my car.

On the way, I stopped at Starbucks and ordered a venti white chocolate mocha and headed to work. Traffic was a mess. I sat back, sipped on my coffee, and listened to Usher sing to me about trading places. I smiled, thinking about the day before. It felt like a dream. My phone rang, shaking me from my thoughts. I hit the button on my steering wheel to answer the call.

"Hello."

"Good morning, beautiful. Why don't you play hooky with me today and let me spend the day with you."

It was Phillip. "Good morning, Phillip. How are you this morning?" I asked him a question so that I could get my thoughts together. Was he playing when he asked me that, or was he serious? Could I miss the day? I quickly grabbed my phone and looked at my calendar. I didn't have any meetings for the day. Nothing pressing that was due. I was smiling from ear to ear. Just to hear his voice and that he wanted to spend time with me, I knew I had to be blushing.

He chuckled. "I take that as a no?"

"Oh, you were serious?" I said, still trying to stall for time. I was still a little hesitant. I didn't want to rush into anything. I didn't want to set myself up for heartbreak again. Something about him was making me bend all my rules that had been two years in the making.

"Yes, baby, I am. Where are you?" he asked. I could hear the smile on his face. He called me baby, and it gave me the chills.

"Well, I'm about twenty minutes from downtown. Traffic is a little bad right now."

"Well, will you play hooky with me today? You haven't answered that yet. Feel free to say no, Maya. No pressure at all. It is a little last minute. But I woke up with you on my mind this morning, and I just couldn't wait to see you." He got quiet. I could hear soft music playing in the background. I turned my music down so that I could hear what he was listening to. It was Kem's song "Share My Life." I smiled.

"Well, sir. I will take the next exit and head home to change. I will call you once I make it home so that we can get our game plan together."

"Yes! That's what I'm talking about. Okay, baby, looking forward to hearing from you and seeing you soon."

I took the next exit and headed back home. I got home in sixteen minutes. I pulled in the garage and quickly disarmed and entered the house.

Once I got upstairs, I called Phillip. I needed to know where we were going so that I knew how to dress.

"You got home fast!" he said and laughed.

"Haha, yes, I did. I wanted to know where we were going so that I could dress for the occasion."

"Well, baby doll. Put on your workout clothes and pack a change of clothes for a long day of walking around, sightseeing. Does that answer your question?"

I laughed. "Yes, it does. So do you want to meet somewhere or what?"

"I can come by and pick you up if that's okay with you. It makes no sense taking two cars."

"Okay, sure." I quickly gave him my address.

We hung up, and I began to change into my workout clothes. I put on a black spandex bodysuit and sports bra and a short blue midriff T-shirt, a pair of socks, and some black-and-blue tennis shoes. I packed a shirt that only had one sleeve on one side and a small strap on the other. The shirt was brown and a pair of brown shorts and some brown tennis shoes and a pair of flat sandals just in case. I also packed another outfit that consisted of a short black dress and some heels just in case we didn't make it back to change for dinner.

As soon as I walked down the steps with my bag, purse, and cell phone and charger, the doorbell rang. I headed over to the table, picked up my keys, and peeked out the peephole. He was looking good.

I opened the door, and we both smiled at each other. "Did you have a hard time finding my house?"

"Actually, no, Maya, when you told me where you lived, I was shocked."

"Why is that?"

"Well, baby, I live a few streets over." He smiled.

"Are you serious, Phillip?"

"Yes. Very!"

"So let's see, that puts you on Pine Orchard Lane?"

"Yes, it does."

"Wow, those homes over on that street are huge. There is this one big, beautiful, two-story house. It puts me in the mind of an antebellum home in Louisiana, with the beautiful wraparound porch. Do you live close to that home?"

He smiled. "That is my home."

"Wow, that is a beautiful home."

"Well, baby doll, you are welcome to come and take a tour. Matter of fact, would you like to do that now on our way to the gym?"

I laughed. "Yes, I would. Would you like to see my home? It's nothing compared to that mini mansion that you are living in, but it's nice."

"Sure," he said, and I moved aside so that he could walk inside.

"Wow, Maya, this is lovely. You have very beautiful mahogany wood floors."

We walked through the downstairs, and I showed him each room, and he asked lots of questions. He seemed impressed.

We headed upstairs.

When we came to the top, I opened the double doors to my room. I heard him gasp.

"Maya, this room is beautiful."

"Thank you. This side of the house used to be two bedrooms and two bathrooms, but I had the walls knocked down and the master bedroom extended." I led him around the room. I opened the door to the sitting area then led him into my master bath. "This is my sanctuary." I pointed out my walk-in shower and huge walk-in closet. Over in the corner was an enclosed toilet. A high-back, clawfoot tub was angled from the window. It took a while, but I finally found it and had it refinished.

We headed down the hall, where I gave him a tour of the two guest bedrooms and the shared adjoining bathroom.

"There used to be two guest bedrooms and two bathrooms, but I wanted the bedrooms to be much bigger, so I knocked out one of the restrooms and opened the rooms up a little more. A shared bathroom gives each bedroom more space."

We headed back downstairs, and he picked up my bag from the floor, and we walked out, laughing like kids and cracking jokes. He opened the passenger door for me, and I slid into his car. On his way around the back side of his car, he opened the trunk and put my bag inside and closed it.

Getting in the car, he looked over at me as he buckled his seat belt. "Maya, it is so good to see you. I know we just saw each other last night, but wow. Do you get more beautiful every day?"

I rolled my eyes at him and laughed. "Phillip, do you get cornier every day?"

We both laughed, and he grabbed my hand. He got serious quickly. His smile melted from his face, and he grabbed my face and pulled me to him. I closed my eyes in anticipation for a kiss on the lips. But instead, he kissed both my cheeks then my nose then my forehead.

"It really is good to see you," he whispered as he looked into my eyes.

"It's good to see you too, Phillip," I whispered in a voice I didn't even recognize.

I quickly cleared my throat. I was uncomfortable. Not a bad uncomfortable. But I hadn't been in this situation in a long time, and I was afraid I would somehow figure out a way to mess it up as I did all my other relationships.

He gently rubbed his hand down my face as he looked from my eyes to my lips. I thought he would kiss me, but he didn't. He turned around and sat back to start the engine.

I leaned back in my seat and let out a slow breath. My heart was racing, and I noticed that I had gotten a little hot. My body was betraying me again. I squeezed my legs together, let out a slow breath, and turned to look out the window. I sucked in a breath when I noticed someone dressed all in black, standing behind a tree on the edge, and between mine and my neighbor's house. I blinked several times, and just as quickly, that person was gone. I shivered because it felt like chills ran up my spine. That was the second time I had seen someone lurking around. I needed to pay more attention to my surroundings. I shook my head quickly to shake those thoughts from my head.

We rode in silence, listening to soft music. Every now and then, we would glance at each other and smile.

"I thought we would go and work out for about an hour if that's okay with you." He smiled as he glanced at me then back at the road.

I laughed. "I don't have a choice, do I?"

"Nah, you said you were hanging with me today. I promise you will enjoy your day."

I smiled because I knew he was right, and I was looking forward to whatever the day held.

We arrived at the gym and got out and headed to the front door. He led the way to the front desk and checked the schedule.

"How about we take a step aerobics class?"

I smiled. "Sure. I'm game."

The next class started in ten minutes, so we decided to go and purchase some bottled water to take to class. We walked in, and there were nine people already there and set up. I walked over to a spot in the back and put my bag in the far corner. I pulled down my step and set it up. He set his step up to the right of me.

I wanted to see his reaction when I took my shirt and sweatpants off, taking me down to a sports bra and some spandex shorts. I kept my eyes on his face as I made it a point to slowly undress. I didn't know what had gotten into me, but I enjoyed the tease show that I was giving him, and by the smile on his face, he enjoyed it too.

He watched me intently. His eyes took in my body from top to bottom, and he smiled. "Very beautiful," he said in a husky voice. He cleared his throat. "Are you ready to get all sweaty?"

We laughed, but before I could respond, the instructor began to speak.

The instructor introduced herself and took us through some stretching exercises, and we began our workout. I kept my eyes on the instructor so that I wouldn't fall and bust my ass. I could see him glancing over at me as we worked out.

We worked out steadily for forty-five minutes, and she took us into a cool down.

After we were done, we all put our steps up and gathered our things.

I was sweating and felt good. Taking a few sips of my water, I looked over at him. He looked as if the workout did not faze him in the least bit. We smiled at each other.

"That was a good workout, Phillip. How often do you work out?"

"I try and get in here five to six days a week early morning. I see you didn't miss a step. How often do you work out?"

"I try and work out six days a week also, but I have a workout room in my house."

"Oh, is that right? Wow, I have a fitness room in my home, but I haven't purchased any equipment. The room is bare."

I smiled. I wasn't sure what to say. I didn't want to be all overly friendly and invite him over to workout in my house every day. It took everything in me not to blurt it out. I was still trying to get to know him, and my workout time was just that, my workout time.

"Well, beautiful, shall we shower and meet at the car?"

"Sounds like a plan." I smiled, and we separated and headed for the gym shower.

I washed my hair and conditioned it. I was smiling as I lathered my body. I was so anxious about spending the day with him I could feel an ache in my stomach. He made me so nervous.

"Calm down, Maya," I whispered, hoping none of the other ladies heard me.

I dried off and wrapped my hair in the towel, applied lotion to my body, sprayed on some body spray, and got dressed. I added some coconut oil and a leave-in conditioner to my hair and pulled my hair up in a ponytail in the back. After packing all my workout clothing in a plastic bag that I found, I walked out to the front. He was sitting in one of the chairs but quickly stood when he saw me approach.

"You are very beautiful," he said as he pulled me into him for a hug and a quick kiss on the lips.

"Thank you. You are looking very handsome yourself," I said and winked. We both laughed.

He had on all brown as if we had planned to match.

"I see you are trying to dress like me, Phillip."

He looked down and stopped before we got to his car. He then glanced at me and fell out laughing. He had on some brown cargo shorts and a brown shirt and some brown shoes. "Wow, Maya. That is too funny!"

He grabbed me again into an embrace and continued laughing. I closed my eyes this time and inhaled his scent. He smelled so clean, and his cologne smelled so good. I could smell the mint on his breath as he continued to roar with laughter. When he released me, I opened my eyes. I sucked in a breath when I saw movement off to the right, and I frowned when I saw a dark figure standing on the side of the building. When that person noticed I was aware of their presence, he backed behind the building, and I was no longer able to see him. Phillip noticed the look on my face and quickly dropped our bags on the ground and grabbed my face in his hands.

I didn't want to spoil the day by telling him about the dark figure, so I refocused on his face.

"Maya, are you okay? You had this look on your face like something was wrong."

The concern on his face and the look in his eyes were shocking. Never had I had anyone show so much concern for me. At that moment, I felt safe with him, and I debated telling him. But just as quickly, I went with my first decision not to.

"Yes," I managed to whisper then cleared my throat. That voice came out hoarse.

He leaned in and hugged me again and kissed me on the lips.

I stood and watched him put our bags in the trunk. He walked around to the passenger side, and I followed and stood back as he opened the door for me.

Once inside the car, he turned and gazed at me. "Maya, are you sure that you are okay?"

I smiled. "Yes, I'm fine, Phillip. Thanks for your concern. So where are we off to now?"

He gazed at me a little longer as if trying to read my expression before he answered. A smile spread across his lips before he did, showing his beautiful white teeth. "We are going to go down to Kemah and walk along the boardwalk. Are you up for some walking? It seems like such a beautiful, windy day for that."

"Sounds like fun." I sat back and buckled my seat belt, and he did the same.

We talked and laughed so much on our ride down to Kemah it only seemed as if we had been riding for a few minutes and not the forty minutes it actually took for us to get there.

At one point, he pulled over to a gas station just to get out and give me a big hug and kiss my neck. This man was giving me so much at once, and I felt as if I couldn't breathe.

Since it was during the week, we had good parking up front. We got out, and he took my hand as we started walking. As we walked in, I stopped and ordered a small cherry slushy, and he ordered the same and paid for it.

"This day is all on me, beautiful."

"Why, thank you, handsome," I said as I did a little curtsy that sent us both into goofy laughter again.

We walked farther in and decided to sit on a bench and look out over the water. We were too engulfed in our slushy and the boats passing by to speak. Once we both finished our slushy, he took and threw away the cups. When he sat back down, he sat closer to me and put his arm around me.

A man came by and took our picture and handed us a claim receipt.

We had no words for that moment. It wasn't too hot or cold, and the wind was blowing off the water, so there was a small chill. With his arm wrapped around me, the chill had no effect.

"Are you hungry?" he said, breaking the comfortable silence.

It was at that moment that I realized that I was starving. "Wow, yes. I'm starving."

"Let's go and eat in the Aquarium."

We stood and walked into the Aquarium, where we were greeted and taken to our seats right away. The perks of visiting Kemah early during the week awarded us quick service.

As we sat, I gazed at the large, floor-to-ceiling aquarium that took up the middle section of the restaurant. I watched the fish swim around, and Phillip did the same. Neither one of us had looked over our menus when the waiter arrived.

"Can you give us a few minutes?" Phillip asked the waiter.

"Sure, sir, I will be back in a moment," the bubbly waiter named Chris said as he bounced off, whistling.

"I guess we should look at the menu," Phillip said and winked at me.

The wink sent shivers down my body. I exhaled and smiled then opened up my menu.

Chris came back, and we gave him our drink and food orders, and he bounced off.

"I am really enjoying your company, Maya. I'm happy that you were able to take this time to spend with me."

"Thanks for inviting me. I really am enjoying this outing," I said and smiled.

"Maya, I remember what you said when we first met. You said you were open for friendship. I must say that after spending this time with you, that is far from what I want from you."

"What do you mean, Phillip?"

"Well, I want you to be mine in every sense of the word. I would like to date you, get to know you, and I want to love you. I want to show you how love should really be."

My eyes widened, and the room got hot. I looked away from his eyes and at the fish in the tank. I looked all around the restaurant and at the faces of others who were there. I looked everywhere but at him. I started fidgeting with my napkin on top of the table. From there, my hands ended in my lap, where I balled them up tightly. My breathing quickened, and I started panicking. I hadn't thought past that moment. I didn't know how to respond. I didn't want to be hurt again, and I didn't want to open my heart up again after I took all this time to mend it only to have it broken again.

"Baby, are you okay?" I hadn't noticed that Phillip had gotten up and sat in the chair next to me. He leaned forward, and he had his hand under my chin. He lifted my face up so that I would meet his eyes.

"Maya, are you okay?"

"Yes. No. Phillip, oh yes, I'm fine," I stammered and closed my eyes.

"Promise me one thing, Maya, and I will do the same. That we will always be completely honest with one another no matter what. I can see that you are not okay, and I am concerned. I really need an honest answer from you."

I exhaled a breath and tried to move my face away, but he held firm to my chin and wouldn't let me look away.

"Yes. I promise," I whispered and closed my eyes.

"Look at me, sweetheart."

I opened my eyes and looked at his lips.

"Look at me, love."

Slowly my eyes met his. "Phillip, I…" Before I could say anything, he pulled me into his lap and hugged me. My body tensed up, but I finally relaxed and put my arms around his neck.

I felt so safe. I felt as if all that I had gone through was okay because I finally had what I had been longing for. Finally, I had someone in my life that truly cared about me enough to help me work through my fears and anxieties. And I finally had someone who wouldn't stop until I was okay. And that was what I felt I would get from Phillip.

I sat up and looked at him, and I leaned down and kissed him softly on his lips. Standing, I sat in my seat. Phillip stood and sat back across from me.

"Maya, tell me what's on your mind."

"Phillip, I've been through so much. I have been single for the past two years. This last relationship really hurt me deep. It has taken all those two years to finally heal. Now here you are, telling me all the things I want to hear and more. I'm scared, and I don't want my heart broken again. I don't really know you, and honestly, I don't know if you are running game."

He flinched as if I had slapped him. I saw pain in his eyes, and he looked away and grimaced. Leaning back, he put both arms in front of him and on the table. I wasn't sure what to do or say, so I decided to just keep silent until he spoke.

"Maya, I've been through a lot too. My heart was broken as well. My ex and I had been dating for four years, and she cheated on me the last year of our relationship with a good friend of ours. I found out because she had a video of her and him having sex saved to our computer."

"Phillip, are you serious?" I said, amazed at why she would do something like that to him, amazed at why anyone would do that to someone.

"I'm very serious. When I let her know that I had found the video, she admitted that they had been sleeping together for a year.

The next day I came home from work, she had moved out. I haven't spoken with her, and I haven't seen her since. So I understand your hesitation with me. And after all that I have been through, you would think that I would proceed with caution. But with you, I don't know. I feel this pull from you. I feel the need to smother you with love, shower you with affection, and love you until you scream."

I sucked in a breath, and we sat, staring into the other's eyes. No emotion. Both of us were in deep thought. We were looking at each other, trying to look deep.

We were snapped out of our gaze by the waiter bringing us our meal. He placed our food in front of us and asked if we needed anything else. We both mumbled no and began to eat.

I thought we were in an awkward moment, and neither knew what to do or say. So eating was the best diversion.

I ate my food without really tasting it, and I never looked up from my plate. Suddenly I lost my appetite, and I pushed my plate forward and leaned back in my chair. Taking a sip of my water, I finally looked at him.

I noticed that he had pushed his plate back and was sitting back, gazing intently at me.

We started our stare again. Phillip broke the silence.

"Maya, I no longer have an appetite. All I want to do is sit with you in my arms."

He didn't wait for my response. He flagged down the waiter. Neither of us wanted to carry leftovers, so we said no to the to-go boxes. Phillip paid for our meal and left a tip. We both stood, and he reached over and grabbed my right hand, and we walked down the steps in silence. Once on the bottom floor of the Aquarium, he stopped. The area was empty.

He turned to me and pulled me to him and kissed me. A light peck at first, then he drew me in to his hungry mouth. The kiss seemed to take my energy away. I moaned, and his grip on me tightened. He moaned as he broke the kiss and hugged me tightly. We stood there for what seemed like hours in a tight embrace.

"Maya, I have no intention of hurting you. I just want to love you. Will you give us a try? Give me the privilege of having you in my life. Bless me with that, please," he whispered this in my ear then kissed and sucked on my neck.

I inhaled a breath through my teeth. He was making me so weak. "Yes, Phillip," I responded in a shaky whisper, and our kiss began again.

He pressed me to him. I felt as if our bodies were one. We were on our own planet, our own island by ourselves. The whole world was shut out. At that moment, it was only Phillip and I. Our breathing, although sporadic, became as one breath. I felt him growing, and I was jarred out of my moment of heaven. I panicked and jumped back and away from his embrace.

Although we were now a couple, I didn't want us to go to that level yet. I glanced away and wrapped my arms around my body.

"Phillip, I…"

"I understand. But, baby, I wasn't looking for that. Our relationship is new. We still need to get to know each other. Sex, me making love to you, that will come in time. But right now, I am content with holding you and kissing you and being near you. But, baby, you know you have that effect on me. My body reacting to you cannot be helped."

I suddenly felt stupid. I was judging him based on others that I had relationships with in the past. With Miles, we just jumped right into sex, never giving us time to grow as friends first before taking that step to sex. I believed that that error in judgment was why we failed. And I really believed that sex was all he wanted, and I settled so that I could have someone in my life. I was startled from my thoughts when I felt Phillip touch my arm.

"Maya, I think we need to go somewhere not so public so that we can talk. I want you in my life, but I don't want to be guessing at what's going on with you. So we can go to your house or my house and sit and have a heart-to-heart. Is that okay?"

I met his eyes. "Yes" was all I could manage to say.

He grabbed my hand, and we walked toward the car.

"I'm going to get our picture," he said and stopped at the picture booth.

I walked over and sat on the bench while he waited behind two other people. I couldn't look away from him, and he kept his concerned eyes on me while he stood in line. He was finally at the counter and gave the lady the claim ticket.

He walked over to me and sat down next to me. Reaching out, he put the picture in front of me. The picture was of us sitting on the bench by the water. His arm was around me, and we were sitting close. Our smiles were big, and we looked so happy. We looked as if we had been together for a long time. The comfort could be seen clearly in that picture.

I smiled and looked over into his eyes. "I'm sorry that I am messing up our day."

"Don't apologize. You are not messing up our day. We will talk about it when we get back. I understand, baby." He stood and reached for my hand. I took it as I stood.

The ride back was quiet. He held my hand the entire trip back. A few times he broke the silence by asking if I was okay. He made every opportunity to touch me in some way, whether it was a touch on the cheek or brushing his hand through my hair, a light squeeze of my leg or arm, or a kiss to his hand to touch my face. He was doing things that made me relax a little more, things that made me question my feelings, my insecure worries.

I put my head down into my hand. I was in deep thought. What would I tell him? How would I explain to him my insecurities? I let out a breath and looked up and realized that we had arrived at his home. I looked over at him, and he was looking at me. His hand reached to touch my face, then he moved to get out of the car.

I waited as he came around and opened my door. Reaching in, he grabbed my hand, and I stepped out.

Once inside his home, he closed the door and locked it and led me into the back part of the house to a living room made up of brown, cream, and red. The matching sofa, love seat, and the four chairs all were overstuffed and looked so comfortable. I contemplated sitting in a chair to keep my distance, but he must have sensed my hesitation and grabbed my hand and pulled me to the love seat.

I sat and sank deep into the cushions of the love seat. It felt as if the love seat was hugging my body, and I relaxed into the comfort.

"Sit and relax, baby. I will be right back." He leaned down and kissed me lightly on the lips and turned and walked from the room.

I took my shoes off and folded my legs under me. Resting my arm on the arm of the love seat, I relaxed. The love seat was angled so that I could look out to the backyard. He had a beautiful, manicured yard. The water in the pool was a beautiful indigo blue. The trees, shrubs, and flowers were beautiful and plenty. I closed my eyes and waited on him to return. Before I knew it, I had drifted off. I didn't know how long I slept, but when I woke, I noticed that I was laying on the sofa and was covered with a blanket.

Slowly sitting up, I looked around the room. Phillip was sitting in one of the big, plush chairs, scooted down and covered with a blanket. He had one hand over his face. I rose and walked toward him, and as I neared, I could hear him snoring lightly. He was so fine and so damn sexy, and my body led me over to him. I didn't know what was coming over me, but I had to be near him. I needed his touch. My body ached to feel his arms around it and his tongue in my mouth. I missed him as if we hadn't seen each other in months.

When I reached his side, I stood, looking down at him, listening to his light snores, and watching the rise and fall of his chest. I was battling with myself. That urge to be with him in that way that I didn't want to happen yet was so strong. But I wanted to feel all of him, every inch of his body on mine. I wanted to feel wanted. I wanted to give him my body. But I knew that that was the wrong thing to do at this early stage of our relationship.

Running my hand down his face, I watched for his reaction. He sucked in a breath, jumped slightly, and moved his hand from his face. Turning his head, his eyes met mine. His hand went to the arm of the chair, and he gazed at me. No words were spoken. No need for words. They would have damaged the moment.

I traced my hand down his face, nails down his chest, then down to his arms. I kept my eyes on his, wanting to capture his reaction to my touch. When my nails trailed his arm, he closed his eyes and moaned, turning his head to the right.

My heartbeat quickened, as did my breathing. I was exciting him, and my touch was turning him on. His moans were proof. I loved that, and I continued running my nails back up his arms then to his chest. I walked over to stand between his legs. My mind said no, screamed no, but I fought past those screams and straddled him. I sat right on his hardness, and I let out a gasp as it grazed between my legs. Chills went up my back, and I leaned my head back as I began to grind into him.

His hands were on my breasts, tracing my nipples, squeezing the whole breast, and I moaned and continued my slowly grind in his lap.

Moaning, he leaned forward and pulled my body toward him. He lifted my shirt up and over my head and pulled my bra to the side to expose my breast, licking and sucking hungrily on my nipple as I grinded in circles and the figure eights in his lap.

In one move, he stood, and I wrapped my legs around his waist. He laid me on the thick carpet on the floor. I could feel the warm, comfortable softness on my back and the cold chill of my arm on the wood floor.

Phillip and I began to kiss again. This time, he was slowly grinding on me. "Maya, I want you so bad. Right now, we are at a point where we can stop before we go too far. But, baby, in a few minutes I won't be able to control myself." He was breathing hard. His breaths sounded like they were getting caught producing strange sounds that were neither animal nor human. They were strange, but they turned me on.

"Phillip, please don't stop."

He didn't wait for me to change my mind. He stood and picked me up and carried me, with my legs wrapped around his waist, to his room down the hall. We licked and sucked on the other's lips while he carried me to his room.

He didn't put me on the bed as I expected. Instead, he carried me into his beautiful bathroom, where he undressed me. I stood naked for a second, but that feeling quickly went away as I was fully aware of how my naked body was making him react. That uncomfortable feeling was no longer a problem as I unwrapped my arms from around my body. I watched this man move around in the bathroom. I realized and understood that shyness was not an option at this point. I was confused at our location and quickly scanned the beautiful bathroom.

He undressed and walked over to the large walk-in-closet-sized shower and turned on the water. Water fell from the ceiling and sprayed from the walls. The room steamed up quickly. As he walked over to me, I looked down. He was very big, and I gasped and quickly looked at his face. He grabbed my hand and pulled me into the shower and closed the glass door. Once in the shower, he stood in front of me and pulled me to him. We began our kiss again, and I put my arms around him. He pulled away and grabbed a towel and began to bathe me. He lathered and soaped up my whole body then put the towel down. Turning me around, he walked me to the wall and began to massage my shoulders, back, and arms.

His touch was igniting fires within me that were out for two years. He was making love to my body, and it wasn't sexual. I moaned and relaxed. My hair was wet, but I was okay with that. The water from the top of the shower washed away the soap and ran down my face and over my eyes.

I wanted to return the favor, and I turned and grabbed the other towel and soaped up his body. I massaged his arms from the front, then walked around, behind him, and massaged his shoulders, back, and arms. I massaged the sides of his neck, moving his head to loosen him up. He moaned, and I could feel him relaxing. Once the water had washed his body clean, I wrung it out and laid his towel down.

He reached over and turned the water from the top of the shower off. He pointed to the shower seat, and I sat. He got down in front of me and pulled me toward his face. I leaned back, waiting for what I knew was about to come. I closed my eyes and let out a loud breath, and I shuddered when his mouth found what it was looking for.

I picked my legs up and wrapped them around his neck and scooted closer to his hungry mouth. So many noises rumbled from my mouth I almost didn't recognize myself. He dined on me, licking and sucking. I felt the waves coming, and I grabbed his head.

They hit, and I sucked in a breath and bucked against his mouth. I moaned his name over and over, and he continued licking on my throbbing and swollen clit. Soon the waves hit again, but this time I couldn't take it anymore, and I pushed back against the wall and away from his mouth.

He stood and leaned into the stream of the water and rinsed his face. There was so much of me on him.

He quickly turned off the water and reached for a towel. Pulling me up from the shower seat, he dried my body and my hair and then himself. Dropping the towels on the floor, he pulled me to him and began licking on my neck. I wrapped my arms around his neck, and he kissed my lips, his hand teasing my nipples. I could feel his erection on my stomach, throbbing and hot. I hugged him tight. My body was screaming for him, all of him.

Picking me up, Phillip walked me to his large bed and laid me down and stood over me. The look on his face was no longer of ecstasy but of something else, something I couldn't figure out.

"Phillip?" I whispered.

CHAPTER 7

Back to Reality

As Phillip drove me back home, I replayed the last twenty minutes in my head. We didn't make love like I wanted.

"Maya, as much as I want to make love to you, I can't and I won't do that to us. I want you so bad, but for now, I can't have you this way."

As we pulled in my driveway, Phillip glanced over at me and half smiled. "Come on, baby, let me walk you to your door."

As we walked up to the front door, he pulled me to him in an embrace and kissed me. That kiss was short-lived, and I was disappointed.

"What's wrong, Phillip? Why are you hesitating? Our previous kisses were much deeper than that."

He smiled then licked his lips. "I'm trying not to get all worked up again. I don't know how to turn off what you do to me. I hope you understand. Our relationship is very important to me, and I want to make sure that I make no mistakes. And, Maya, we never had our heart-to-heart. That is a conversation that we have to have soon, baby."

I smiled and hugged him tight. "I understand, and yes, I know. We will plan on that."

I watched as Phillip pulled from the driveway, and I watched until I could no longer see the light from his car. Before I could close the door, I caught movement to the right of my garage. I almost screamed and backed into the house and quickly closed and locked the door. My hands were reaching for the alarm system, and I quickly alarmed the house. I moved toward the nearest window and looked all around for that dark figure. Just as quickly, that person was gone. I was frightened but felt safe with the house alarmed.

Walking into the kitchen, I put my bag and purse on the barstool and stood and leaned on the counter. My phone began vibrating in my pocket, and I quickly reached to answer it, almost dropping it to the floor.

"Hello."

"Oh, you finally answer your phone! Homegirl, where the hell have you been?"

Hearing her voice calmed me, and I relaxed into the call.

"Hi, Vicki, it's so nice to hear from you, cousin. How was your day? Did you make it home safely?"

"What the hell? Maya, are you okay?" Vicki's tone softened.

"Yeah, I'm okay, Vicki. I spent the day with Phillip."

There was silence on the phone. Then I heard a loud scream.

"YES! FINALLY, YOU FOUND A MAN TO OCCUPY YOUR TIME!"

I laughed. "Really, Vicki, I needed a man to occupy my time? I don't think so."

We talked for about thirty minutes. I replayed my day with her, from his phone call that morning to when he dropped me off. I decided not to tell her about the dark figure I had been seeing.

"Wow. So he seemed different?"

"Yeah, I mean I don't really know him that well to read him. All I can say is, my feelings are a little hurt. I feel like the relationship is ending before it has gotten started."

"No, I don't think you should look at it like that. Phillip is a nice guy. Derrick speaks highly of him. So I think things will be just fine. Just enjoy him. Take things slow, and don't go into it with your heart. Go into it thinking of building a friendship. Leave sex out of the equation. Sex complicates things, especially if it is had too early in the relationship. Everything will be okay, cousin. And if not, I will definitely whip his ass."

We both laughed. After we hung up, I got ready for bed and watched a movie until it watched me.

CHAPTER

8

Party Time

The rest of the week went by pretty slowly. Every day and night I heard or saw Phillip. We made it a point to have dinner together every night. Everything seemed to be fine with us, and Monday was never spoken of. We got to know each other, never going past the heavy kissing and hugging.

Vicki and I shopped off and on throughout the week for the dinner party. Finally, Friday came, and after work, Vicki came over with her overnight bag.

We got up early that Saturday morning and began preparations, cleaning my house from top to bottom and prepping the hors d'oeuvres.

"Girl, you have been too damn quiet. What the hell is on your mind? I know it's not the party tonight."

"Oh, Vicki, I'm good, girl. It's just been a busy week with the preparations for the party. I'm a little tired. If I could, I would cancel the party now so that I can get some rest."

Vicki stopped arranging the flowers and turned to look at me. Putting her hand on her hip, she frowned. "Maya, say what? Girl, get a glass of wine or something. Perk up. We are about to have some fun. Think about that chocolate thang you got coming over here. Speaking of, have you spoken with him since Monday?"

"You know I have. I don't know why you asked. I speak with and see him every day. I am trying to keep my distance, but I feel a little pull. I feel like I will drop my guard too soon with him. He is so easy to talk to. He is funny, smart, and seems to have his head on right. I just don't know."

"Maya, it has been two years since Miles. If that chocolate man is pulling at your heartstrings, girl, let him! Ha!"

"I hear you, Vicki," I said, shaking my head. I was shaking my head, but my body was saying yes.

The phone rang, and Vicki reached to answer it. "Hello. Oh, sure thing, hold on a second. Um, Maya, it's Phillip."

Grabbing the phone from her, I suddenly got nervous. "Hello," I said with a shaky voice.

"Hello, beautiful. I was calling to say hello, hear your voice, and to see if you needed me to come over and help you with anything."

"Hi, Phillip, that is so sweet of you. No, my cousin is here, helping me out. We already have the food pre-prepped. We are just putting the finishing touches on the decorations. We will be done with that in the next hour."

"Okay. I guess my plan at seeing you before the crowd is a no go?"

I leaned on the counter and closed my eyes. If that man came over, I would be so nervous I might break something or burn the food. But he might be what I needed in order to wake up. I was so sleepy and needed a boost. He did know how to make me laugh.

"Well, just come on over. Bring what you will wear tonight and come over and hang with me and Vicki."

He laughed. "Are you sure, beautiful?"

"Yeah, I'm sure."

"Okay, beautiful. I will see you in a few."

We hung up, and I let out a breath. "That voice and that man have me swooning!"

"When I answered the phone, I was thinking, *Damn!*"

We gave each other high fives and laughed.

"I'm not trying to be the third wheel, Maya, so I'm calling my baby to come over too."

"Girl, do whatever you want. I'm going to wash my face and make sure I look okay."

I almost forgot that Phillip lived just a few streets over. The doorbell rang ten minutes after our phone call.

I heard Vicki yell that she was getting the door, and I continued washing my face then looking through my closet for something to wear. I decided to ask Phillip what he was wearing so that I could match him. Then I quickly thought against that and chose a black blouse that did not have sleeves but tied around the neck and exposed most of my back and a pair of cream-colored slacks and some tiger-print high heels.

"Maya, Phillip is here!" I heard Vicki yell.

"Okay, make yourself at home, Phillip!" I yelled down the hall. "I will be there in a second."

I heard the doorbell ring again and knew that Vicki would get it.

For the moment, I chose some black short shorts and a red halter top and some gold flat sandals.

When I walked into the kitchen area, Derrick and Phillip were sitting at the bar, cracking up at something Vicki said.

Phillip was the first to see me and stood and quickly walked over to me. He hugged me close and kissed me like he hadn't seen me in months.

"Hey, baby," he said and smiled.

"Hey," I said and smiled back.

"Hey, cut that mess out. You don't see Derrick and I all over each other like that."

We all laughed, and I walked over to stand next to Vicki while Phillip took his seat.

The room was filled with laughter and food smells. We had everything set up, food in the steamers, wine and champagne on ice. The sink was filled with ice and beer, juice, and soda. Cups were near, and the plates and forks were placed next to the food steamers.

All that was left for us to do was to get dressed.

"Well, I guess we can get dressed. Phillip, you can change in my room. Please follow me, sir."

He and I walked down the hall and up the stairs, laughing and holding hands.

Both of us had already bathed, so we just sat in the chairs next to the window and talked.

"Come and sit in my lap, sexy," Phillip said and smiled a seductive smile.

I walked over and sat in his lap.

We kissed and hugged for what seemed like hours. We ended up on the bed. The kissing and rolling around on the bed were getting me so worked up. I couldn't breathe, and the friction was really working me up. We pulled away, breathing heavily, when we heard the doorbell downstairs.

We sat, staring at each other like a deer in headlights, until I heard my cousin yell that she had the door. Both of us let out a breath, and Phillip rolled off me.

"I guess we need to get up and get dressed, Phillip."

"I just want to lay up here with you, baby. Do you think they would miss us?"

We both laughed so hard after that.

Phillip rolled onto his stomach and was positioned with his lips close to mine. He leaned in and kissed me softly, and I moaned. We started again. As he angled his head to the right, I parted my lips to let in his tongue. His hand found my breast, and he squeezed.

Sucking in a breath, I moaned and rolled my body toward his.

"Maya, Phillip, people are starting to arrive," my cousin yelled as she banged on the door.

We both pulled away from each other and stood.

"How about taking a cold shower with me, Phillip?"

He grabbed and adjusted the bulge in his pants and shook his head yes.

We both quickly undressed and showered, helping each other wash the other's back. Once out of the shower, we quickly toweled off and retreated to separate sinks to brush our teeth. I did my normal ritual with my hair and makeup, glancing at him off and on. We shared smiles and blushes.

The room was silent except for us moving around.

I went into my closet to put on my clothes, and he retreated into the bedroom to dress.

I sprayed my favorite perfume then leaned down to fasten my shoes. I put on my earrings, watch, and bracelet. I walked from the closet and walked toward my room.

He was standing with his hands in his pockets, fidgeting, hopping from one foot to the other. The room smelled of him, and I closed my eyes for a second as I inhaled his scent. He looked so handsome. I took him in from head to toe—sexy.

His eyes lit up when he noticed that I had walked into the room, and he dropped his hands down to his sides. "You look so beautiful. I am so anxious to show everyone my beautiful woman."

I smiled. I was lucky and very happy.

"You look very handsome, Phillip," I said as I winked at him and smiled.

He returned my smile and pulled me to him. We embraced and pulled apart quickly.

"You smell so good, Phillip."

"Thanks, baby, so do you."

We walked down the steps, hand in hand. When we got downstairs, everyone had arrived. I noticed the frown on Kiera's face when she saw me that came and went when Daren jerked on her arm slightly. He had a strange expression on his face. The darkness in his hazel eyes told the story. What was odd to me was, I saw the same expression on Derrick's face. I frowned, and they both cleared their throats and pasted on a fake smile. Their eyes were still dark.

We all began to mingle and eat and drink. The party seemed a success. Everyone was laughing and seemed to be enjoying themselves.

I walked into the kitchen to make sure there were enough drinks on ice in the sink and didn't notice that Daren had followed me. I turned and almost bumped into him.

"You look so beautiful, Maya. Are you and Phillip together?" he said as a disgusted look came across his face.

"Thank you, Daren. You and Kiera look very nice. And, yes, Phillip and I are together."

Before I knew it, he had grabbed my wrist and pulled me out the side door. Once outside, he closed the door and turned to me.

I jerked my wrist from his tight grip. I grabbed my wrist, which felt hot, and rubbed it. I knew it would be bruised in the morning.

"What the hell is wrong with you, Daren!" I raised my voice at him and put my hand on my hip.

"Really, Maya. First, you get with me. Now you are with Phillip? Why are you trying to hurt me? Why are you doing this to me?"

He had tears in his eyes, and every word brought him closer to me. Once he was on me, he shoved me up against the wall. It knocked the wind out of me, and suddenly I was scared. The look in his eyes was frightening. His hands were on my shoulders, squeezing tight. Every time he talked, he pushed me into the wall, and my head hit the brick.

"What is wrong with you? Let me go!" I yelled, hoping someone would hear my pleas.

"I love you with everything in me. And I promise you, I will hurt you before I let anyone take you from me!"

"What are you talking about? We are not together! We never were! We talked about this! You and Kiera are together! Go back in there with her and move on!" I pushed his hands from my shoulders and turned to walk away. He grabbed my arm again and jerked me toward him. I stumbled and almost fell. Grabbing me by the back of my head, he leaned in until our lips almost touched. I struggled, but it was no use. He was strong, and his grip never wavered.

"You heard me, you little teasing bitch. I will hurt you before I let anyone else have what's mine!"

"I am not yours, you idiot! You and Kiera need to leave my house. Now!" I screamed. I had tears streaming down my face as I walked into the kitchen. I headed for the bathroom in my office. On the way, I met Phillip's eyes, and he followed me.

I sat on the edge of the tub and rocked. The wild look in Daren's eyes had me scared. The way he slung me around had me shaken up. I could smell alcohol on him, but I couldn't blame the alcohol for this. My stomach lurched, and I felt as if I would throw up. Grabbing my mouth, I jumped up and headed for the toilet. All I could do was dry heave. Nothing came up. A thought flashed in my head. I was

CHAOS

wondering if he was the dark figure I had been seeing. My breathing was hard as I continued to dry heave.

I was startled by the banging on the door.

"Maya, open this door!" I had closed and locked the door. I didn't know what to tell Phillip. How would I explain this situation with Daren?

I sat back down on the edge of the tub and rocked and cried. Somehow, Phillip found a way in.

"Baby, what is wrong? Did Daren hurt you?"

"Yes!" I yelled and jumped up and into his arms.

He was shaking as he led me into my office, where he wiped the tears from my eyes and the snot from my nose.

"Baby, I will be right back."

It was silent, and I heard yelling, and I heard a glass shatter and a scream.

I jumped up and ran into the front. Phillip had Daren by his throat and had him lifted off the floor. The scream was from Kiera as she tried desperately to get Phillip to put Daren down. But her screams and hits to his large arms went unnoticed. Derrick was talking calmly to Phillip, trying to get him to put him down. Derrick cut his eyes over to me and then quickly looked back at his brother.

I walked over and gently placed my hand on his arm. "Baby, put him down please. He is not worth getting in trouble for."

And just that quickly, Daren was dropped to the floor. Kiera quickly helped him up.

"Daren, get the hell out of my house!" I yelled.

"I knew I shouldn't have come over here to your house, you stupid bitch…"

Before Kiera could get all her words out, I slapped her across the face. She looked shocked and stumbled back against the wall. She looked at Phillip and smirked then rolled her eyes.

"Get out of my house, you thirsty little bitch!"

They both turned and left. But before Daren could get out the door, he turned to me.

"Remember what I said, Maya!" He looked from me to Phillip and smirked.

Phillip lunged at him, and I grabbed his arm to calm him.

Derrick grabbed my arm, jerking me around to face him. I jerked my hand from his grip.

"Get your damn hands off me, Derrick! And you can get the hell out of my house too!"

"Maya, what the hell happened?" His eyes quickly went to my chest and arms. I didn't notice that large black-and-blue marks had already started to appear. "Maya, did my brother do that to you?"

"Yes, he did. Something is wrong with Daren. He is not himself. He told me that he would hurt me before he lets anyone have me," I cried as Phillip held me. My friend had turned on me. That in itself hurt me so bad.

"Maya, I'm sorry. I will go and talk to my brother. I don't know what's wrong with him, but I promise you that he will never hurt you."

I looked into Derrick's eyes and saw sadness. His green eyes watered. I touched his arm. "Derrick, I never thought that he would hurt me, but look at the bruises on my arms and chest. I love your brother as if he was family, but I no longer want him in my life. He is a loose cannon." After I said what I had to say, I grabbed Derrick and hugged him.

Derrick and Vicki walked past me, and as Vicki passed, she grabbed me and hugged me. She had been crying. "I love you, cousin. I feel like this is my fault because I urged you to invite them. I am so sorry."

"I love you too, Vicki. You had good intentions. Don't beat yourself up about this. What happened had nothing to do with you."

My house cleared out quickly. All that was left was the broken glass on the floor and silence. Phillip and I just sat on the sofa. No words were spoken while he held me. After what seemed like hours, he finally spoke.

"Maya, what happened?"

I sat up and moved from his arms. I looked down and closed my eyes. I was dreading this question, but I knew that he would ask.

"Please don't judge me when I tell you. Please. Promise me you won't." My eyes were pleading with him. I put my head down into my hands and took a deep breath. I was waiting for him to answer.

"Maya. I won't judge you."

"Promise me, Phillip, that you won't let this harm our relationship."

"Maya, I don't like the sound of this. But I will tell you this, I do not like mess. And what happened here tonight, I don't like that either."

"Okay, I won't make you promise. Phillip, Daren and I have been friends since we were kids. And he has always had a crush on me. He has always been there for me as a good friend. When I was dating Miles, Daren and I stopped hanging out. He always had something to say about what Miles was doing or who he was doing. He always wanted to talk about how Miles was not good for me. So I stopped hanging out with him, stopped calling him, and stopped answering his phone calls. Pretty soon he got the hint and stopped."

I paused and looked at his face. There was no reaction. I couldn't read him. So I decided to continue.

"Just in the past year, Daren and I had started mending our friendship. The day that I met you at their parents' house, um, well." I got stuck. I was stumbling over my words. I was embarrassed and ashamed for repeating what I was about to say to Phillip. I didn't want him to be disgusted with me, and I didn't want this to mess up our relationship.

"Maya, go ahead and tell me," Phillip said. His voice was soft and filled with understanding.

I looked at his eyes. I still could not read him. Dropping my head down, I looked at the sofa and began to dig my nails into the fabric.

Phillip grabbed my hand. "Maya, we have to be able to be honest with each other. We need to be able to talk to one another. Okay, baby?"

I nodded and began again.

"The day that I met you, Daren and I had had a conversation about hanging out. He was pushing to date me. He wanted me to feel for him what he felt for me. I told him that that would never happen, but I was okay with us hanging out. The subject of us being friends with benefits came up, and after some thought and a little coercion, I decided to allow it. He said he would keep his feelings separate, and if he felt that he could no longer do that, then he would let me know." I stopped again and looked up and into Phillip's eyes for a reaction.

I saw something there that I'd never seen before. I decided to go ahead and just get it out. I was stalling, and it needed to stop. I owed him that much.

"Well, one thing led to another, and I slept with him that day. Afterward he told me that he couldn't handle it. Daren said that he loved me more than ever. Said that he would be there for me, and if I ever decided to let him love me, then he would be there. When you walked me out, him and Kiera were in the kitchen, hugged up, kissing. I felt relief. I thought, *Good, I'm glad he has someone to fall back on.*"

Pausing, I looked up from the pillow that I was pressing my hand into and into his eyes. He was frowning, but his face softened as he looked into my eyes.

"Phillip, you have this look on your face. I can't explain it. But you don't look pleased with me. I didn't cheat on you, and I've never been dishonest with you."

"I know, Maya, but the thought of another man touching you pisses me off. Is there any more to this story?"

"Well, after you went back into the house, Daren came outside. He told me not to worry, that he was okay, no hard feelings, and that he and Kiera would be together. He walked away. The next day, Daren came by my house. Said he wanted to apologize for the night before. We talked for a little bit. I invited him and his girlfriend to the party, and after that he left."

"No more invites for him or her. We will just keep our distance. If you hear anything from him, let me know. I'm not going to do anything, but I have some police buddies. I will call them and ask what our next step would be. Okay, Maya?"

I relaxed. It felt good to have someone take control and make sure that I was okay. "Okay."

"Let's get the house in order and get some sleep. I am going to stay here for the next couple of days to make sure we won't have any problems from him."

I smiled and shook my head. He pulled me to him and hugged me tight and kissed my lips.

"Are you okay? Those bruises look bad," he said, gently touching the ones on my chest.

"No worries. They look worse than they really are. They are just really sore."

After we cleaned the house, we checked to make sure all the windows and doors were closed and locked. Phillip went outside and checked the perimeter of the house. When he came back in, I alarmed the house, and we headed upstairs.

We took a quick shower together. Both of us were in deep thought. We quickly dried off, dressed, and climbed into bed. It was not all that late, so I turned the TV on. I laid my head on his chest, and he draped his arm across my back. Every so often, he would rub up and down my back and kiss my head.

CHAPTER 9

Not as It Seems

I didn't remember falling asleep, but when I opened my eyes, it was bright in the room. I slowly rose from Phillip's chest and glanced at the clock, and it read 7:50 a.m. When I glanced over at Phillip, his eyes were open, and he was gazing at me. I smiled, and he returned my smile.

"Good morning," he said and grabbed my arm and pulled me toward him.

"Good morning," I said before he kissed me.

We kissed deeply, and we slowly laid our heads back onto the pillows. He pressed his body into mine, and I could feel his manhood poking me in my stomach. I wanted him so badly. My body was hot, and I could feel the moisture between my legs. The softness of the sheets and the feel of him touching my body sent chills through me. I was going crazy, and the only thing that would help was to be able to make love to him.

He rolled on top of me, and we did a slow grind. We were both moaning and out of breath when he broke our grind and rolled off me.

"Maya, damn. This is getting hard. I'm going crazy."

I wanted to tell him that it was okay, that we could make love. But I wanted to hold out. I wanted—no, needed—to wait until it was right. Kicking the covers off me, I tried to allow my body to cool off. We were both breathing hard.

"I know, Phillip, so am I."

CHAOS

He got up and went into the bathroom and closed the door. After a few minutes, I heard the water turn on in the shower.

I laid there and slid my hand down into my panties and gave myself a much-needed release. By the time my body stopped shaking, the water in the shower turned off. I quickly rose from the bed and made it. When he came out, he looked more relaxed. He probably gave himself a much-needed relief too. I smiled at that thought. He smiled.

He grabbed me as I headed into the bathroom and gave me a big hug. He was totally nude, and my body started heating up again when I pressed against him. I quickly pulled away, but he held me tight and kissed me. The kiss was deeper than any that we had had before and left me weak. He grabbed me by my butt and pulled me closer. We were panting when we pulled apart.

We just stood there, staring into each other's eyes. The desire in his eyes sent chills up my spine.

We pulled apart, and I walked past him and into the bathroom. He swatted me on the behind, and I turned and looked at him and smiled as I closed the door.

When I got out of the shower, I paused. I could hear him talking, and he sounded a little angry. His voice was muffled, but I could have sworn that I heard him ask someone why they were with Daren. I slowly walked to the door and stood still and stopped breathing so that I could make out every word.

"Well, she just got out of the shower, so I will call you later."

After that, there was no sound, just the voices on the TV.

I quickly dressed and walked into the room. He was dressed and sitting in the chair next to the window. His face held a look of aggravation, but just as quickly, it was gone, and a smile spread across his face when I walked closer to him.

I decided not to ask him about his phone call. Time would only tell. I was just glad that I hadn't slept with him. I knew things were too good to be true. That phone call I heard gave me the feeling that he was talking with Kiera.

I was pissed because I had been on the up and up with him. But something just didn't seem right. Things were too good to be true.

I didn't return his smile right away, and he picked up on that. "What's wrong, baby?"

"Oh, nothing. I'm just a little hungry. I will go down and make us some breakfast."

"I will help," he said, jumping up from his seat.

We walked down the stairs in silence. He put his arm around me and kissed the side of my face and smiled. I smiled in return.

We ate breakfast, and he helped me clean and put away the dishes.

"Baby, I hate to leave, but I need to get home and get situated. I need to take care of some errands and return some phone calls. Maybe we can get together for dinner." He smiled as he pulled me to him. He kissed me lightly on the lips then sucked on my bottom lip. He kissed down to my neck, where he lightly kissed and sucked.

"That sounds good, Phillip." I smiled at him, and he hugged me again.

When he left, I grabbed a bottle of water and my phone and sat on the couch in the living room. After dialing Vicki's number, I turned on the TV and began to surf the channels while I waited for her to pick up. She didn't answer. She must be with Derrick. I hung up without leaving a message.

I sat in deep thought as I tried to replay the conversation with Phillip that I overheard. I was stressing myself out, trying to figure it out. I didn't know what to do. I needed to talk to my cousin, and fast.

Shaking it off, I opened my water and drank. I found a movie on cable and got lost in it. About thirty minutes into the movie, my phone rang.

"Hello."

"Hey, cousin, are you okay?"

"Yeah, I'm good. Why do you sound so down? What's wrong?" My cousin sounded sad. It was very unusual for her.

"What's wrong, Vicki? Did something happen after you left last night?"

"Yeah, it's been a mess. I'm coming by your house. I just left Derrick. I will tell you about it when I get there."

We both hung up without saying goodbye. My stomach was now in knots. What could have happened? I decided to ditch the water bottle and go open a bottle of wine to breathe. I knew whatever was going on, Vicki would want to have a drink with me. After that I made a sandwich tray because I knew my cousin would be hungry. I laid out smoked turkey and cheese, olives, pickles, and little cups of mustard and mayonnaise. I placed a bag of Doritos on the tray for Vicki and some sour cream and onion chips for me. I placed that tray on the table in the living room. Glancing at my watch, I slowly sat and tried to watch more of the movie.

Twenty minutes later, I heard Vicki come through the front door. She never did that even though she had access to my house, so I knew something was wrong. I jumped up and ran to meet her.

"Vicki?" I grabbed her and hugged her. She looked as if she had been crying.

"It's just been a crazy night and morning, Maya. I have never seen Daren act like he acted last night. He and Kiera came by Derrick's place last night, and it was not pretty."

"Wow, what happened? Come sit down. I have a bottle of wine ready and a light lunch."

We walked into the living room. Vicki placed her purse in the chair and sat next to me on the couch. I reached for the remote and muted the TV.

"When we got to Derrick's house, he was so mad at his brother. He was pacing the floor, saying he didn't think he would lose it like that again over a woman. That freaked me out, since that was the first that I had heard of it. He told me that Daren used to date this woman and ended up engaged to her. He saw her out with some guy and went ballistic. After punching the guy, he forcefully put her in his car and took her to his house. When they got to his house, he beat that girl within inches of her life. Told her the same thing that he told you, that he would hurt her before he let anyone else have her. Later it came out that the guy was her cousin. He had just come in town to visit the family and surprised her at work and took her to lunch. Daren had been following her. He ended up spending about eight months in jail."

"Oh my god, Vicki, are you serious?" I was so scared, and now it was confirmed that Daren was the dark figure that had been popping up.

"Yes! When he told me that, I was so scared for you, and I let Derrick know, and he said the same. He said he was frightened for you as well. Maya, I don't want him to hurt you like he did that girl. Derrick said he broke her nose. She couldn't see from one of her eyes, broke a few teeth from her mouth, broke her arm, and a few of her fingers. Her face was so bruised that her own family couldn't recognize her. She ended up leaving Texas. Derrick and his family are unsure of where she went."

"Vicki, all of a sudden, I'm frightened. I've been seeing this dark figure popping up. I saw this figure all dressed in black outside my job when Phillip came to bring me dinner weeks ago, by the tree between mine and my neighbor's house, and at the gym when Phillip and I went to work out. Who knows the other times I may have missed seeing him?"

"When did this all happen? Daren and I have been friends for years. I don't understand. It's like he is two different people. There is this other side of him that I know nothing about. It's like he lives a double life. I am so thrown off right now because I don't know what Daren is capable of. I don't like feeling like this. Like my whole life is out of my hands."

"Calm down, cousin. Derrick is trying to take care of this. When we got home last night, Derrick called his brother and told him to stop by, they needed to have a talk. He did, and when he walked through the door, Kiera was with him. And she looked scared, Maya. She really did."

"I really hope he doesn't do anything to her. I don't care for Kiera, but I don't wish anything bad on her either. What happened after they got to Derrick's house?"

"Well, Derrick started yelling at him. Told him that he better not start that crazy shit again. He asked him if he wanted to go back to jail, and he said no. At one point, Daren dropped down to the ground and started crying hysterically. I felt bad for him. Kiera backed away and ended up sitting in a chair. Daren told Derrick how much he loved you and said he couldn't turn that off. At that point, Kiera jumped up and walked over to him. She told him that she couldn't be with him if he was so in love with you. She walked out of the house. I don't know if or how she got home."

"Okay, so what else happened? You aren't telling me anything to make me feel as if this whole situation is handled."

"Derrick was able to calm Daren down. He talked to him for so long that I fell asleep. When I woke up and looked at the clock, two hours had passed. Derrick and Daren were sitting on the couch, and Daren was very calm. He told him that he wouldn't bother you and asked Derrick to apologize to you. He said that he was going to take a vacation and go away for two weeks to clear his head."

"I don't know, Vicki. I am still getting bad vibes. I just don't know."

"Don't worry, Maya. Everything will be okay. Just don't worry. Do you mind if I spend the night here, Maya? I'm so tired I just want to shower and crash."

"Go ahead. It's so early though. It's only 5:15 p.m. But I understand it was a long, exhausting night." I got up and hugged my cousin. She gulped her glass of wine then got up and headed down the hall to the guest room.

I sat and sipped on my wine and watched some television. Actually, the TV watched me. I just couldn't shake the creepy feeling that Daren was somewhere close by.

I had forgotten all about Phillip until the phone rang, jarring me from my thoughts. I hurried to answer it so that it wouldn't wake Vicki.

"Hey, babe, I was thinking about you. Do you want to come over and spend the night with me?"

"Hey, Phillip, no. Vicki is here. She went to get a shower and get some rest. I just want to hang around in case she needs me. I hope you understand."

"Yeah, I understand. As long as you aren't there alone, I'm okay with that. Well, call me if you need me. I'm going to catch up on some work." Right before I hung up with Phillip, I heard his doorbell ring. The phone hung up before I could hear anything else.

I fought with myself not to put on my tennis shoes and walk over to his house to see who it was. After that phone call that I overheard, he was now on my shit list.

I decided against it. I wasn't up to finding anything else that would hurt me at this time.

After I cleaned up the tray and wineglasses, I alarmed the house and cut off all the lights. I decided to look out the front window because paranoia had set. It was dark, but I could see a car parked across the street. The car almost looked like Daren's. I turned and ran up the stairs so that I could get a better look at it from my bedroom window. When I looked out the window, the car was gone. A cold chill went up my spine, and I quickly closed the blinds and closed all the curtains in the room. I stood there and held myself as I shivered.

Walking softly back down the stairs, I peeked in on my cousin. She was snoring lightly, so I knew she was tired. Closing the door, I headed to the kitchen for a glass of wine; I needed something to calm me so that I could sleep.

I tossed and turned all night, dozing and waking at every little sound. At 4:45 a.m., I decided to get up and get dressed and work out. Maybe that would help.

After about an hour, I decided to shower and get ready for work. On my way back upstairs, I peeked in on my cousin. She was sitting on the side of the bed, but she was dressed.

"Hey, Vicki, good morning. Are you okay?"

"Oh yeah, just trying to fully wake up. How are you? Were you able to get some rest?"

"No, not really. I tossed and turned all night. Every little sound woke me up. I finally decided to get up and work out around 4:45. I checked on you last night, and you were knocked out, snoring. I'm sure you needed that rest."

"Yeah, it was just so much. Seeing someone that I thought of as a brother totally change to someone that I've never seen before really has done something to me. It was very sad for me. Feels like I lost a friend."

"Yeah, I know how you are feeling. Do you want some breakfast?"

"No, I'm going to head on home so that I can get ready for work." Vicki stood and walked over to me and gave me a big hug.

"Call me if you need me. If you don't want to be here by yourself, you can come and stay with me, or I can come here. Whatever you need, cousin, I'm there for you. I love you."

"Thanks, Vicki. I love you too. I'm okay. Don't worry so much. I think the only thing that we can do for Daren is just pray for him."

After Vicki left, I alarmed the house and went and looked out the window. I couldn't get it out of my head that I saw Daren's car parked in front of my house last night. I felt that chill and quickly shook it off. I didn't see any other strange cars out front, so I relaxed a little.

Once I got to work, I focused on my workload. When I finally decided to take a break, I realized that I never touched my breakfast, and I was very hungry. I called my assistant and asked her to get me a California club sandwich and fruit from Jason's Deli.

It took about forty-five minutes before it came, but I decided to close my office door and have lunch at the table. That way, I wouldn't be tempted to start working again and end up not eating.

As I sat and ate, I realized that I hadn't heard from Phillip that day. It was 12:45 p.m. I refused to call him; that was just not me. I focused on eating and my much-needed break. I kicked my heels off and picked up my phone.

The phone beeped, indicating a call from my assistant.

"Hi, Jessica. What can I do for you?"

"Hi, Maya. You have a delivery. Shall I bring it in?"

I was confused. I wasn't expecting anything.

"Sure, Jessica, bring it in." I hung up the phone and turned to face the door.

Jessica walked in, carrying a large brown and green vase with so many roses. It looked as if the vase would tip over from the weight of the roses.

"Wow" was all I could say as I got up to accept the vase from her.

"You have something else, Maya. Let me go out and get it." She turned and walked from my office.

Leaning in, before I made contact with a rose, I could smell how fragrant it was.

I turned just in time to see Jessica walking in with another vase overflowing with calla lilies.

"Oh wow, my favorite!" I whispered as Jessica put them on the table.

"Both have a card, Maya," Jessica said through a smile as she walked from my office and closed the door.

I pulled the card from the roses and read it.

> *To the most beautiful woman in the world,*
> *The flowers are just because I'm happy to be your man.*
>
> *Phillip*

I smiled and walked over to the vase of calla lilies and read the card.

> *Missing you.*
>
> *Phillip*

I didn't remember ever getting flowers from anyone, and this beautiful gesture had me near tears. Picking up my phone and scrolling through my contacts, I called Phillip.

He didn't say hello, just answered the phone with a question. I could hear the smile in his voice.

"So you got my flowers, beautiful?"

I smiled and giggled like a stupid schoolgirl. "I did. Thank you so much. They are beautiful, absolutely gorgeous. I love them."

"I'm glad you like them. How about we have dinner tonight, love?"

"Sure. Come by the house, and I will cook for you."

"Okay, sweetheart, see you tonight. Can't wait to see your face and kiss your lips." He didn't wait for me to respond. He hung up.

I sat down and quickly finished my lunch and got back to work. I had some things to complete before I went home.

CHAPTER 10

Romantic Evening

I decided to make Phillip a meal he wouldn't forget. Sausage and shrimp jambalaya, fried corn bread, and peach cobbler and vanilla ice cream. I had just taken the cobbler out of the oven when the doorbell rang.

I ran to the door and peeped out the side window. The night before was still fresh on my mind, and I still used caution when opening my door.

Opening the door, I could feel the breeze whip in, carrying with it his smell. Phillip and I smiled at each other. I moved to let him in and closed the door. As soon as the door closed, he pulled me in for a big hug and a kiss that had me weak in my knees.

"You smell so good, Phillip," I said between kisses.

He squeezed my butt as he pressed his body to mine. "Baby, you always smell good. And, wow, the food smells so good. I'm starving."

He grabbed my hand, and I walked him into the dining room. I had set up the dining room intimately with candles. I had a bottle of white wine sitting in an ice bucket, chilling.

"Please, Phillip, have a seat. I will bring you your plate."

"Wow, I get special treatment. Thanks!" he said as he smacked me on the butt when I turned to walk away.

I giggled and walked into the kitchen to fix our bowls of jambalaya and salad. I put them on a serving platter, along with matching saucers, with buttery, fried corn bread and hot sauce just in case he needed a kick. But I was pretty sure that he wouldn't because I made the jambalaya extra spicy.

When I walked back into the room with the server, Phillip rose from his seat to help me. Placing the platter on the side table, I sat.

"Would you like to bless the food, Phillip?"

He smiled, and we bowed our heads.

"Heavenly Father, thank You for this food that we are about to receive. May it strengthen and nourish our bodies. I ask that You bless the hands that prepared it. In all these things we ask in Jesus's name. Amen."

"Amen," I said then looked at him. "Phillip, the jambalaya is spicy. I just wanted to warn you." I smiled as his eyes grew big.

"I love spicy food, Maya, and can't wait to taste it. Everything looks so good." With that, he dug in and began to eat as if he hadn't eaten in years.

I began to eat as well, focusing on the bowl in front of me. It was good, probably my best, and I was waiting on him to say something about it. Finally, he did.

"Maya, baby. This is so good."

He had cleaned his bowl, and I was only half done with my meal. I laughed.

"I made dessert. Do you have space for dessert?"

"Baby, I would like another bowl of this jambalaya, and, yes, I have plenty of room for dessert."

I rose to go and get him more, but he held his hand out.

"Baby, finish your meal. I can get it."

I smiled. "Okay."

I could see him fixing his second helping, and he was smiling. He all but ran back to the room to sit down and eat.

I smiled and finally finished my food and sat back to watch him.

"How was your day?" he managed to say between bites of food.

"Very busy day. What about you?"

He exhaled before he answered as if he had a rough day. "It was busy and rough."

We sat and talked, then I served dessert. We ate the peach cobbler in silence until he commented.

"Maya, this has to be the best peach cobbler that I've ever tasted. Wow! Dinner was amazing. If I eat like this every night, I will be four times my size." We laughed.

"Thanks for the compliment. My mother taught me well." I smiled.

"Yes, she did," he said and leaned over to kiss me lightly on the lips and swat me playfully on the butt.

I cleared the table and put the dishes in the dishwasher as Phillip made himself comfortable in the living room.

I could feel myself relaxing with him again, and I was really enjoying his company. I couldn't shake that phone call I heard, but I didn't want to dwell on that any longer. I loved being around him, and I knew, in no time, my heart would open to him. I think I would actually fall in love with him.

We sat and talked and laughed, and between the laughter and the talking, we kissed and hugged. This man was drawing me into him, and I loved the attention that he gave.

"Maya, I really feel like you are the one. I know we haven't known each other long, but, wow, I feel like you have me falling. I'm scared to say falling in love because it's too soon."

"Phillip, I was thinking the same thing."

I didn't want to say too much else, so I left my comment at that. I did decide right then and there to put that phone call that I had heard from my mind. I didn't want to keep dwelling on it. What was done in the dark would come to the light. If there was something that I should know, I was sure I would find out.

Six months later—all in love

Time had gone by so fast. Philip and I were working a lot but always managed to spend time together. It seemed that we had shut the world out. It was me, him, and work.

I was sitting at my desk, and my phone rang, shaking me from the contract that I was looking over. I jumped and dropped the folder onto the floor, spilling out everything in it.

"This is Maya," I said while crawling around on the floor, putting the folder back in order.

"Hi, baby."

I smiled when I heard his voice. Six months later, and the sound of Phillip's voice still gave me chills.

"Hey, you," I said, grinning hard and giggling.

"Are you all ready for our trip?"

It was Thursday, and Phillip and I had planned a weekend getaway to New Orleans to celebrate our six-month anniversary. Both of us had shared a cab to our respective jobs, loaded down with our luggage for the trip. A rental car would be delivered to Phillip at 1:00 p.m., and he would come pick me up.

I glanced at the clock and noticed that it was 1:15 p.m. I panicked because time had gone by so fast.

"Phillip, wow, time has gotten past me. Is it that time already, baby?"

"Yes, I'm downstairs, in front of the building, waiting for you. Come on down, baby. Let's go have some fun."

"Okay, baby, I'm on my way down."

I hung up the phone and sprinted to my assistant's desk and gave her the folder with the new contract and instructions on phone calls and emails that I needed her to take care of. Fifteen minutes later, I was riding down the elevator with my luggage, running things through my head to make sure I hadn't forgotten anything.

Once I exited the glass door in front of the building, I saw Phillip emerge from a silver Cadillac Escalade. He walked over to me and planted and big kiss on my forehead and grabbed all my luggage and placed it in the back of the truck.

Once the bags were loaded, he turned to me and gave me a big hug and one of his kisses. He always kissed me as if he hadn't seen me in years. In the beginning, it would bother me because no matter where we were, or who we were in front of, he always made it seem as if we were the only people on the planet in that moment. As time had passed, I learned to appreciate his affection.

When we pulled apart, as usual, we were both out of breath. He swatted me on the butt as I turned to walk to the passenger side of the truck. As always, he opened the door for me and waited for me to buckle up before he closed the door.

The whole drive to New Orleans, we talked, sang, and had so much fun, enjoying each other's company. I was so excited that we had scheduled this getaway. It was much needed.

We held hands, and every now and then, he would lean over to me and ask for a kiss.

In these past months, despite our work schedule, I really got a chance to know him. I knew that I was in love with him but hadn't told him. He hadn't said anything either. We still had not made love, but we had planned on it this weekend, and I was a nervous wreck.

We finally arrived in New Orleans and pulled up to the hotel to valet park. After settling in our room, we decided to set out on foot to get something to eat.

"Baby, let's eat at Ralph and Kacoo's," I said, excited to be in New Orleans again.

"I was going to suggest the same thing," he said, grinning.

We walked hand in hand, taking in New Orleans, passing over Bourbon Street, and finally to our destination. The smell of food led us the rest of the way. I didn't realize that I was starving, and my stomach was making very strange noises. Phillip overheard and laughed while he hugged me.

"We will eat soon, sweetheart," he said and kissed me on the lips.

"I hope so, baby, because I am beyond starving."

We were seated within minutes of us arriving. The restaurant wasn't packed, I thought as I smiled, looking around the familiar room. It was dark and romantic. Everyone was friendly and held big, welcoming smiles.

In our excitement about our trip, we talked nonstop about New Orleans. During our conversation, I found out that both of us had been several times, and we both loved eating at Ralph and Kacoo's.

"I was thinking that we would just hang out and rest in our room tonight. We can get up and go have breakfast in the morning and walk around and buy souvenirs. By then, it should be lunchtime, and we can figure out where we can eat then. Walk some more and take pictures, have dinner, then come back to the hotel and rest.

Change clothes, then hit Bourbon Street around ten. What do you think, love?"

"Wow, Phillip, you have our day planned out. It all sounds good to me. I can't wait!"

We were sitting by the window, so we talked and people-watched. We kissed throughout dinner and fed each other food. I was sure people watching us were either sick of seeing our display or happy for the cute, happy couple.

On the way back to the hotel, we stopped at a little corner store and bought some water and snacks for our night of resting.

When we made it back to the hotel, we took turns showering and dressing for bed. It was only 6:45 p.m., but we wanted to relax and watch a movie while relaxing in the bed.

I showered first and got comfortable in the bed. I decided to wear something different, other than my normal white T-shirt and boy shorts. I was wearing a little satin top with spaghetti straps that tied in the back and was long enough to fall just above my butt. The top was black and revealing. I wore a thong on underneath. I had on a black satin robe when I walked in the room. He kissed me on the cheek and smacked me on the butt then went into the restroom to shower. I took the robe off and slid into bed and pulled the covers up so that he couldn't see what I was wearing.

He finally walked into the room and put away his dirty clothing. I watched him move around. The sight of his naked skin made me flush, and I looked away, but not before taking him in from head to toe. He had on some black satin boxers. I smiled. It seemed as if we were both on the same page with the black satin.

He climbed into bed, and I leaned forward to allow him to put his arm around me. After we moved pillows around and adjusted, we finally found a comfortable spot.

Phillip grabbed the remote from the table next to the bed. "You have any idea the type of movie you want to watch, baby? I'm sure it's some sort of chick flick or love story, right, baby?"

We laughed, and he hugged me and kissed me lightly on the forehead. There was so much sexual energy in the room it caused us both to be uncomfortable and fidgety.

CHAOS

After channel surfing, we decided to order a movie. We both decided on *Jumping the Broom*. We started the movie and talked a little until it began. He reached over and turned the lamp off then wrapped his arm around me.

My heart was beating so fast. Lying next to him made me so nervous. We had spent several nights and weekends together, so my nervousness had nothing to do with newness. It had to do with me knowing what was to happen, what was going to happen, before the night was over.

Phillip leaned over and kissed me on the forehead and ran his hand through my hair. I wasn't ready yet. I needed time to relax. But it was a false alarm. He turned and focused on the movie.

I was surprised that we made it through the movie without anything happening. We snuggled the whole movie, and he lightly kissed my lips halfway through the movie.

"Do you want to watch another movie, baby, or are you ready to call it a night?"

"I guess since we have such a busy day tomorrow, we should call it a night."

After turning off the TV, he hooked up his iPhone and started softly playing music. When I heard Anthony Hamilton's "I'll Wait to Fall in Love," I smiled and scooted down in the bed.

I was laying on my back, and he was laying on his side, with his arm around my waist. His face pressed into mine. He began planting light kisses on my face. His right hand found my face, and he ran his hand down and then back up and into my hair. I closed my eyes. The feel of him next to me was driving me nuts.

When his lips found my neck, he pressed his body on my leg. I could feel him growing, and it was now on top of my leg. I moaned when he found and kissed that spot on my neck that turned me on.

Our lips finally met, and we started kissing so deeply and passionately I could hear my soul take a deep breath then sigh. He rolled on top of me, and I opened my legs to make room for him.

My body was so warm, and I was so wet. I wrapped my arms around his neck then placed my hands on his back. I rubbed down his back with my hands, then back up gently with my nails. He moaned, and we began our normal slow grind that had been getting us through these long, sexless months. But this time, we were going all the way. Before we would grind until both of us would collapse from the friction and extra work.

His hand found my right breast, and he put his full hand on it and began to squeeze then flicked his thumb across my nipple, which sent chills through my body. My nipples were my other hot spot, a spot that could make me cum without having to be penetrated.

He broke our kiss, and his lips found my neck, where he gently sucked, causing me to shiver and dig my nails deeply into his back. I wrapped my legs around his waist and moaned when I could feel his manhood graze my clit. I began to utter that long, drawn-out, unbroken line of the letter *S*.

"Sssssssss. Oh, Phillip, yes," I whispered.

"You like that?" he whispered.

"Yes, baby."

His mouth found mine, and we kissed. He was the best kisser. He broke our kiss and quickly lifted my top over my head then pulled the thong off and threw them to the floor. He then pulled off his boxers and threw them to the floor.

He began kissing down my neck then sucking until his tongue found my nipple. He licked and sucked, and I moaned and grinded into him. I was ready, but he was taking his time tasting my body.

Wrapping my legs over his shoulder, he began to taste me, and I grinded into his face. I was anxious for a release, and I grinded faster and faster while holding his head with both hands. Just as I was about to get there, he pulled away. My body shivered.

He reached over and pulled out a Magnum condom and rolled it over his rock-hard and thick penis.

Rolling on top of me, he didn't enter me. We began to kiss again. I wrapped my legs around his waist and braced myself. He rubbed on my clit with his hand as he positioned his penis at my opening. He was big, and I could feel it stretching me. But it felt so good. I opened my legs wide as he slowly entered me.

I took in a deep breath, and my eyes opened to look into his face. He paused once he had entered me all the way, and we kissed.

His hand found my nipple again, and he tweaked it. I moaned. My excitement had me breathing very irregularly. My moaning was loud, and I was calling his name over and over.

He started slowly grinding, and I grinded with him. The feel of him inside me was pure heaven. He made love to my body from top to bottom. He pulled out before I could finally have my release.

"Turn over, baby."

I rolled over and onto my knees. Grabbing my hips, he entered me, and we began to grind. He laid across my back and played with my nipples while he kissed and licked my neck and down my back.

He pulled out again and got up from the bed. He pulled me by my leg to the edge of the bed; our lovemaking was getting a little wild. And I loved every minute of it.

We made love all over that room. Finally, while I was riding him in the chair, I had my release. He picked me up and walked me back to the bed while holding me, with my legs wrapped around him. We kissed. And when he laid me down, we began our slow grind again. This time, he found my G-spot, and I came hard, and he came with me, pausing while we both were racked with shivers.

He never moved. We starting kissing while we hugged each other tightly.

"I love you, Maya. I love you so, so much," he whispered.

I opened my eyes and looked into his. "I love you too."

We got up and showered together then got back in the bed. We didn't put anything on this time, both slept in the nude.

Sleep came fast, but I was awakened by him licking my clit. We made love again then showered. We fell asleep quickly.

I woke before him, around 4:15 a.m., and woke him by sucking on his manhood. Again, we made love and fell asleep, holding each other tight.

We slept until 8:45 a.m., when we heard the tap on the door announcing the housekeeper had arrived to clean our room. Phillip jumped up and ran to the door and cracked it just to let her know we were still asleep. He put the Do Not Disturb sign on the door then closed and locked it.

I closed my eyes. I was so tired from our night and wanted to go back to sleep.

My eyes snapped open when the covers were snatched from me and I was pulled to the edge of the bed. Phillip dropped to his knees and began to lick and suck on my clit. I moaned and squeezed the sheets tightly in my hands. My release was quick, and I squeezed my knees, trapping his head between my legs. He wouldn't stop his licking, and my body jerked again. This time, I pushed him away.

He climbed over me and guided me onto the bed where he slowly made love to me. We both came together, breathing hard and weak.

Rolling off me, Phillip laid next to me and wrapped his arm around my shoulder.

"Baby, we need to get up and to get something to eat. I am so weak, and I don't have any energy."

"Okay" was all I could manage to say. I was weak too but didn't have the energy to express that.

We slowly made our way to the bathroom where we showered. We didn't have the energy at that point to do anything but bathe.

We found a restaurant not too far from the hotel to eat breakfast, where we both ordered so much food, deciding on certain dishes so that we could share. When our food arrived, we sat and ate like savages. A couple at the table next to us glanced at us and giggled.

We didn't care and kept eating. We sipped on coffee after eating and gazed out the window. Neither of us had said a word. To me, there seemed to be a change. I was sure it was because we had slept together.

I quickly glanced at him only to find that he was sipping his coffee and staring at me.

Sitting forward, I grabbed my coffee cup and began to drink, never taking my eyes off his.

"I am enjoying this time with you, Maya. I really am. And what I said last night, about me loving you so, so much, I do. I love you so, so much. You have my heart. All I ask is that you don't break it."

I smiled and waited a moment before responding. "And I am enjoying this time with you, Phillip. I know you meant it. I love you too. And I mean that as well. I won't break your heart if you won't break mine."

We both laughed.

After Phillip paid the check, we started walking around, going in and out of stores, buying souvenirs for friends and family. We laughed and talked and held hands. Finally making it to a place where we could sit, we stopped and looked over the water. We held hands and talked.

I realized that my phone was ringing, and I quickly dug it out of my pocket. It was Vicki.

"Hi, cousin, how are you?"

"Hey, Maya, sorry to cut your trip short, but someone broke into your house. I am here with the police."

"What! Are you serious, Vicki!"

"Yes. Maya, you and Phillip should get back as soon as you can. Whoever it was had some nasty words spray-painted on the floor and walls of your kitchen and living room. They trashed your room. But nothing appears to be missing. The police say that it looks like the vandalism was personal. Maya, seriously, this has Daren written all over it. I'm sorry to cut your trip short."

I had grabbed Phillip's hand and yanked him up from his seat. "Vicki, we need to check out of the hotel, and we are hitting the road. Thanks for calling, cousin. Love you."

"I love you too. Please be careful."

"Maya, what's wrong?"

"Phillip, someone broke into my home and vandalized it. We have to get back to Houston now, baby."

"Okay."

After packing our bags and checking out of the hotel, we loaded our bags and left. Stopping quickly to fill up the car, we finally hit the road. The trip seemed to take so long. It seemed as if we had been on the road for twelve hours, but we finally made it.

When we entered the Houston city limits, I decided to call Vicki. I had already spoken to her several times on the trip home, but I wanted to let her know that I was minutes from home.

"I'm still at your house, Maya. Derrick came over and is helping me pick up broken glass and haul the trash out."

"Okay, Vicki, thanks. See you soon."

When we arrived at my home, my stomach was in knots. I got out of the car and ran toward the front door.

When I walked inside, I began to cry loudly.

I felt an arm around my waist and one around my shoulder. I couldn't tell who the arms belonged to because the tears clouded my vision. Closing my eyes and squeezing them tight, I ran both hands across my face.

Vicki had one arm around my waist, and Derrick had his arm around my shoulder.

"I'm okay," I said through sobs, and they let me go.

The lamps in the living room were smashed. The TV was bashed in and pushed onto the floor. The bookshelf was pushed over, and books and pictures sat swimming in broken glass. Glass was everywhere. On the wall close to the door, there was graffiti, and it read:

> *You thought you could get rid of me. Remember what I said!*

I gasped and took a step back. I turned and looked at Derrick.

"Yeah, I'm pretty sure my brother did that. I'm sorry, Maya. I let the cops know what had transpired at your party and that I think that he may have done that. Truth is, Mom and Dad and I haven't heard from or seen him since the day after your party. It's been six months. I don't understand."

I walked away from Derrick and into the kitchen. All the cabinets were open, and every glass, plate, bowl, serving dish, and coffee mug was broken to pieces onto the kitchen floor.

I turned and walked up the stairs to my bedroom. When I walked into my room, I had to stop and steady myself. The bed was turned over, and the walls looked like they had been kicked in and hammered. There were large holes all over the walls. The curtains and blinds had been yanked down. The TV was smashed and laying on the ground. I peeked in the bathroom and the sitting room, and there was no damage.

I turned, and Phillip was there, and he reached out for me. He held me as I cried.

"You cannot stay here. Pack your clothes and toiletries. I'm taking you home with me until you can get your home back to the way it was."

"No, this is my home. No one is going to run me from my home."

At that moment, Vicki came in.

"Vicki, did the police say how this person got in?"

"There was no forced entry, and the alarm code was keyed in. Whoever it was came in through the front door."

I closed my eyes and opened them.

"Derrick and I are not leaving your side until all this mess is cleaned. However long it takes, Maya."

"Yeah, and I'm not leaving either. We can get it done quickly with all of us pitching in," Phillip said as he squeezed my arm.

We all got to work, starting downstairs, sweeping up and picking up broken items and putting them in heavy-duty trash bags. Phillip had pulled the large trash can to the front door so that we didn't have that far to walk.

A few hours had passed, and we had everything picked up. The broken TVs were on the curb for heavy trash. Phillip found some paint in the garage and primed and painted the graffiti on the wall in the living room. My house was looking back to its old self, except for the glass missing from the picture frames and the missing TVs and the missing lamps that were smashed. My bedroom would have to be done professionally. Derrick had called his father, and he and one of his friends were coming over the next morning to assess the damage and do the work. Until then, all I could do was just close the door.

I went over and sat on the couch with the phone book and made two calls, one to Pizza Hut and one to the Chinese restaurant down the street. Vicki sat next to me, and Derrick sat in one chair, and Phillip sat on the arm of the sofa next to me. He rubbed my back as I put the orders in for food.

"You okay, Maya?" Phillip said as he moved the hair from my face. He placed his hand on my back and rubbed. It was making me relax a little.

"Yeah, just a little sad about the damage Daren did to my home. I worked hard to make my house into a home, and all he did was destroy it. I feel violated. My heart hurts because I had forgiven him for what he did the night at the party. Now this happens. Why did he wait six months? All this makes no sense to me."

I looked at Derrick, and his face held sadness. Vicki went over and put his arm around him, and he smiled a smile that never made it to his eyes.

"I don't know what to say, Maya. I've tried calling him only to reach his voicemail as I have been doing for the past six months. My parents have been doing the same. We've even called Kiera, and she hasn't heard from him and said that she has moved on. I've gone by his home, but no answer. I can't even tell if he is in there. The lawn people cut his grass like clockwork. I don't know. I really think you should go downtown and file an order of protection against him. I don't know what's on my brother's mind. All I know is, I don't want him to do to you what he did to his ex-girlfriend. He put that young lady through so much," Derrick said through clenched teeth. He put his head down into his hands and exhaled loudly.

"Yeah, I thought about that too. I will go and get the order of protection first thing Monday morning. I'm not sure how he got the code to the front door, but I will put a new code in so that he can't use it again. I do have a firearm if he decides to come back. I'm not scared, so I have no problem staying in my house. All the security features help. I just have to make sure that I use all of them now," I said as I looked up at Phillip.

"Don't worry, baby. I will help you get everything secured in here," Phillip said as he leaned down and kissed my forehead.

At that moment, Phillip's phone rang, and he dug into his pocket and pulled it out. I watched his face as he looked at the number flashing on his screen. He looked around and jumped up.

"I'm going to take this outside," he mumbled then dashed for the door.

We all looked at each other and frowned.

"What the hell was that about?" Vicki loudly whispered.

"I don't know," I mumbled. All of a sudden, I was getting that feeling. That red flag was up, and this time, I would not ignore it.

I got up and tiptoed to the door and leaned my head forward. Phillip was arguing with someone, and I could only make out a few words. I heard him say, "No, you are not coming over here." He then said, "You will not tell her that." I heard him let out a huge breath, then he said, "Yeah, okay, I will see you tonight at 8:30 to talk, but then you have to go."

I turned and went and sat back on the couch, and I quickly looked over at my cousin. "Vicki, something is not right."

Before she could say anything, Phillip came back in the house, and behind him was the pizza delivery and the Chinese food delivery. I jumped up to go pay.

"I got this, baby, don't worry," Phillip said as he paid the delivery drivers and handed me the food.

I kept my eyes on his face. He never could look at me. He was avoiding me. He was guilty of something, and tonight at 8:30 p.m., I was going to find out. I cut my eyes at him and looked over at Vicki. She and Derrick were walking toward me into the kitchen.

Setting the food down, I went into the pantry and pulled out some paper plates, napkins, and plastic forks and knives.

We all sat at the kitchen table and started fixing our plates and eating. There was nothing but silence.

Getting up from the table, I went to the fridge and pulled out a pitcher of iced tea and got the paper cups from the cabinet next to the fridge.

I began pouring tea for everyone then sat down to finish eating. I realized that it had started getting dark, and I looked at the time. It was 8:15 p.m. I turned and looked at Phillip, who was checking the time as well. He looked at me quickly then back down to his plate. I wasn't sure about his eyes. They held something, guilt maybe, I thought as I frowned at him.

"Baby, I have to go home for about an hour, but I will be back with some things so that I can spend the night here with you."

"Okay, Phillip." I stood as he stood and walked him to the door.

He hugged me and kissed me quickly on the lips then walked out of the door. I watched out the window until I saw him leave, then I sprinted over to where my cousin sat.

"Vicki, I'm going to walk over to Phillip's house and see what's going on. Someone is coming to see him at 8:30, and I need to see what's going on."

"Do you want Derrick and me to go with you?" my cousin said, looking worried.

"Maya, do you think you should be doing that? I don't want you looking for danger," Derrick said with wide eyes.

"Derrick, I love you both, but I need to find out for my peace of mind. I promise I am not looking for danger, and I will be right back."

I turned and ran toward the front door then down the driveway. I started speed-walking once I reached the corner, making sure to stay in the shadows that the trees cast on the sidewalk. It took me less than five minutes to make it to his house. His car was in the driveway, and the lights were on in the front part of the house. I stopped walking and looked around, making sure no one was outside, watching me. When I felt that they weren't, I walked over to the gate leading to his backyard and gently pulled it open and walked in and slowly pulled it closed. It barely made noise, but I paused to listen just in case.

I walked slowly up the sidewalk and around to the back of his house. I could see the light shining from the back of the house. My heart was pumping so fast, and I realized that I was breathing hard, so I stopped walking to slow it. Taking in slow breaths, I could feel my heart rate and breathing slowing down. At that moment, I heard a car pull up, and the door open and slammed. I could hear the *click, click* of shoes on the driveway, then banging on the front door.

I quickly made my way to the back of the house and found a spot behind a huge tree. I remembered the tree from when I was sitting in his house, looking out. I remembered thinking how huge it was. I hoped they chose this room to talk so that I could see who it was. I stood waiting, and finally, I saw him walk in first. He walked in and stood in front of the patio doors with his hands on his hips. I couldn't see who was in there with him, but I finally heard a voice. It was loud, it was female, and it sounded familiar. I frowned, trying to catch that voice.

He lunged forward and put his hand on the door to steady himself, as if he was pushed, and he turned quickly, and there she was. My mouth was wide open. It couldn't be. What in the hell was she doing in Phillip's house? Why was Kiera at Phillip's house?

I moved slowly around the back of the tree and closer to the house. Once I did that, I could hear them clearly.

"What do you want, Kiera? It has been over between us for a while now. What could you possibly need to talk to me about?"

"Really, Phillip, you and I slept together last week. Now, all of a sudden, it's been a while. Wow, does your bitch know that you have been sleeping with me while she was holding out on you?"

"Kiera, what we were doing is over!"

"Oh, it's over? So on your little love trip to New Orleans, she must have opened her legs for you. Aww, that is so sweet. Darling, you and I will be over when I say it's over. I'm enjoying this. I never liked that little bitch. And now I can finally say that I had something of hers, and I had him first!" Her smile was wide. The look on her face was of one who had won millions. She was enjoying this.

"Like I said, this thing between you and I is over!"

Kiera slowly walked over to Phillip, and his hands dropped from his hips.

With her right hand, she reached and grazed her hand across his manhood then squeezed. He flinched and stepped back, but he had a smile on his face. I sucked in a breath as my anger was growing.

"See, you enjoy our playtime just as much as I do. You can never leave this alone," she said to him as she walked around him then stopped again in front of him.

Kiera walked closer to him and cupped her hand to his manhood and began to massage. He grabbed her arm and dragged her over to the couch, where he pulled her pants down and bent her over. He quickly dropped his pants, and without using protection, he entered her. She squealed and moaned as he leaned down and raised her shirt up and over her head. Grabbing her breasts, he began his slow grind into her then he pulled out and turned her around and pushed her down on the couch. He got down on his knees and pulled her to his face and began to taste her. She moaned and grabbed his head.

My stomach lurched as I watched in disgust. I could feel tears falling down my face, but I couldn't pull myself from my spot. I couldn't believe what I was seeing. How could a man who said he loved me so, so much make love to another woman? That mouth that was tasting her was, only hours before, kissing and tasting me. That sent me over the top as I leaned over and silently threw up my dinner next to the tree. After I regained my strength, I focused again on the sickening display.

She grabbed his head and pushed him away, and he stood as she stood. She pushed him down on the couch and mounted him and began to ride him. I could see his face, and now I wanted him to see mine.

Stepping around the back of the tree, I walked up to the door. I watched his face as he realized that I was there. His mouth fell open, and he pushed Kiera off his lap and ran toward the door.

"Maya, oh my god, Maya, please let me explain," he said as he opened the door.

I diverted my eyes and looked over at his whore as she walked up behind him. She was smiling. She didn't even try to put on any clothing. She stood there naked and proud—proud of the mess she had created. I cut my eyes at her and turned to him.

"Wow, Phillip. You love me so, so much, huh? So, so much that you could hurt me so, so bad. You know what I've been through in my past relationship with him cheating. You expressed to me how your ex cheated on you. We also talked about not hurting each other. But you managed to do just that. Hurt me. I hope you enjoy your little whore. Everyone has passed her around. I don't ever want to see you again as long as I live. You don't exist to me anymore." I turned to walk away, and he grabbed my arm. I turned and looked at his face and snatched my arm from him.

"Don't you ever touch me again." I turned and walked around the back of the house then to the street and back to my home.

When I walked in the front door, Vicki ran over to me. "Maya, why are you crying? What happened?"

"I went over and made it there before his guest. I watched them from the backyard. He had sex with her. Then I stepped out from where I was hiding so that he could see me," I said through shaky tears. Suddenly the room began to spin. I was seeing stars. Then I saw darkness.

"Who!" Derrick said as he grabbed me before I fell.

I had passed out. With the mixture of today's activities, I was exhausted mentally and physically. When I came to, I was laying on the couch, and Vicki was wiping my face with a cool towel, and she was crying softly.

"Vicki?"

"Maya, how do you feel?"

"I'm okay, just tired. My heart is so broken, Vicki," I said and began to cry again.

"Calm down, Maya, please."

"I'm calm. I'm just hurting."

"Maya, you said that he had sex with her. Who is her?" Derrick said from his sitting place in the chair.

"Kiera," I whispered.

"What!" Vicki said as she jumped up and reached for her phone.

I sat up and grabbed her. "Vicki, don't call her. If you are calling Kiera, please don't. She can have him. And I don't want her to have the satisfaction of knowing that I am hurting. You should have seen that smug smile on her face as she stood there naked."

Vicki slowly sat down on the couch next to me and placed her phone on the coffee table. I heard Derrick let out a hard breath.

Vicki put her arm around my neck, and I leaned my head on her shoulder and began to cry.

After what seemed like hours, I sat up. "Vicki, you and Derrick don't have to stay here with me. I am fine. I want to be by myself anyway."

"Maya, I don't want to leave you here alone."

"Don't worry, Vicki. I will be fine."

"Let me check all the windows and doors before I go," Derrick said as he walked toward the stairs.

"Okay, thanks, Derrick."

"Maya, are you sure?"

"Yes. I will call you in the morning. Don't worry, I will be fine."

After Derrick and Vicki left, I took it upon myself to recheck the doors and the windows. I went to the door and rekeyed a new code then to the security pad and armed the house.

I decided to sleep in my office since it had a futon and headed that way. All I could do was collapse and pull the blanket around me. I fell asleep fast and slept straight through until I heard the doorbell. I rolled over and looked at the time on my phone. It was 2:45 a.m. Who in the world could it be at this time of the morning? I slowly rose and crept down the hall. Once I got to the window in the kitchen, I peeped out without disturbing the blinds. It was Phillip. He rang the doorbell about nine times before setting out down the driveway and to the sidewalk. I watched him until I couldn't see him anymore.

I dragged myself back to the office and laid down. I was asleep before my head hit the pillow.

I was awakened again by my phone ringing. It was 3:30 a.m. "Hello."

"Maya, I'm sorry. I don't know what to say…"

I hung up before Phillip could say anything else.

Minutes later, it rang again, and I put it on silent and turned over and fell back to sleep.

I was awakened again by the doorbell and loud banging on the door. This time, I decided to open the door and let him in.

Never looking at him, I stepped back so that he could come in. "Maya…"

"Phillip, I'm tired. Say whatever you have to say and leave. This is the only reason I let you in. So once you have said what you have to say, leave and never darken my doorstep again. I don't want to hear from or see you again. And if you come around again, I will go downtown and put an order of protection on you."

I paused and finally met his eyes. I could see the hurt. He had on the same clothes from earlier that day, and he smelled of alcohol. I had never smelled him like this, and my stomach turned with every exhale that he took. He had been crying.

"Maya," he said with a shaky voice. "I love you so much. I know that I can't possibly explain this away. I know that I have hurt you, and for that, I am so sorry. But, baby, please don't throw us away. Whatever you want me to do to fix this, just tell me. I will," he said through sobs.

He was crying, and I was not moved. A part of me, for just a second, wanted to pull him to me and hold him and tell him that we could work through this, but I couldn't. Because if I forgave him and we moved on, it was highly possible that he would do it again.

"Maya, please say something," he said as he dropped to his knees in front of me and hugged my legs.

I stood there for a second, and I quickly pushed him back. He sat on the floor with his head in his hands and sobbed.

"Phillip, if you have nothing else to say, please leave my house."

"Oh baby, please." He said words almost hard to understand.

"Bye, Phillip," I said through clenched teeth.

He slowly rose from the floor. When he leaned in to kiss me, I quickly pushed him back and stepped away from him. "Don't kiss me with lips that you just had on her," I spat, bile rising in my throat. "Leave my house before I call the cops."

He nodded, and with head down, he walked out of my door and out of my life. I closed the door, bolted it, and reset the alarm.

I cried from the front door until I fell asleep. My heart once again was broken. I wasn't sure if it could be repaired this time. I ached for Phillip; my body longed for him. Over time, that ache and that longing would subside.

CHAPTER

11

Ghost from the Past

When I finally opened my eyes and looked at the clock, it was 10:15 a.m. Groaning, I rolled over to sit up and smooth my hair from my face. Derrick's father was coming by at 11:30 a.m., and I needed to get up and get a shower and get dressed.

I showered and tamed my hair. After fixing a quick breakfast, I made myself a large cup of black coffee. By the time I ate and cleared the dishes, the doorbell rang.

"Hey, Maya, I'm so sorry about everything you are going through right now. I don't know what's wrong with my son. I don't understand where his mom and I failed with him," Derrick's father said as he gave me a big hug and squeezed.

"Thank you for coming doing this work for me, Mr. Clark. Please let me know the cost, and I will gladly take care of it," I said, not wanting to talk about Daren.

"Maya, considering that my son did this, you have no worries. I will handle the cost. This is my buddy, Gregg Daniels."

I stopped and my eyes got wide. Could it be? Was I standing face-to-face with Miles's father. I gasped and took a step back.

"Maya! I haven't seen you in years! How have you been?"

"Mr. Daniels. Yes, it's been a long time. I'm okay, considering the events that have transpired lately. How is Mrs. Daniels?"

"Oh, she is fine. I will tell her you asked about her. She brings your name up a lot. Before I leave, I will have to get your number so that she can call you," he said in his Louisiana accent as he leaned down to give me a big hug.

He didn't mention Miles, and neither did I. That was a name best left unspoken. I had enough going on and didn't want to add to it. Although I was sure Mr. Daniels would be calling Miles when he left my house. Damn.

I let Mr. Daniels and Mr. Clark upstairs to my bedroom and swung the door open.

"Oh no. Look at this mess," Mr. Clark said as he placed a hand on his hip.

"Yeah" was all I could manage to say as I choked back tears.

"Okay, Maya, Gregg and I are on the job. We brought food and water, so no need to worry about us."

"Okay, Mr. Clark. Please let me know if you need me. I am going to be in the guest room downstairs, laying down. I am really tired."

I walked downstairs and to the guest room and got in the bed. I was tired, and that futon in the office only made me sore.

I slept for what seemed like hours and woke to the doorbell. I rose and stretched. I felt much better. Walking down the hallway and getting closer to the door, I could hear Mr. Daniels and Mr. Clark talking. The doorbell rang again, and I quickly moved toward the window to look out. It was Vicki, and I sprinted to the door to let her in.

"Why didn't you use your key, Vicki?"

"I don't know. My mind is not all the way there." Her face held sadness.

She walked in then pulled me to her in a tight embrace. Nothing was said. She reached up and pushed my hair from my face.

"Cousin, are you okay? Have you eaten? I brought us some food."

Placing the bags on the breakfast table, Vicki began to unpack them. And the aroma from the containers hit me, and my stomach growled.

"Is that Boudreaux's?"

"Yes, I got your favorite pasta. Sit down and eat. I heard your stomach, and I know you are hungry."

I sat and watched my cousin busy herself, laying out the food in front of me and for herself, then she sat.

I realized my hair was everywhere, and I pushed it from my face and put it into a ponytail. I met Vicki's gaze.

"Cousin, I don't know what to say. The night before just seems so unreal. Your heart must be so broken."

"I'm okay. And this too shall pass. I can't sit and dwell on this. Yes, I'm hurting, and I'm so tired of hurting. This is the main reason I didn't want to get involved with anyone. I was trying to guard my heart. It won't happen again. I can promise you that."

"Don't count love out, Maya. You just need some healing time. But please don't harden your heart."

I looked at my cousin and gave her a small smile, or so I thought, then began to eat.

We ate in silence then looked out at the birds on the front yard.

"I'm going to check on Mr. Daniels and Mr. Clark," I told Vicki as I stood.

"Mr. Daniels? As in Miles?"

"Yes. I was shocked when I realized who he was. I just hope he doesn't bring my name up to Miles. That is one ghost I want to remain in the past."

Vicki and I cleared the table and walked up the stairs. Mr. Clark and Mr. Daniels were packing up their things, and my room looked almost normal. They had covered everything with plastic and had sheet rocked and floated the walls. No more holes.

"Wow. You guys did a beautiful job."

"Thanks," they both said through big smiles.

"Maya, it needs about a day to dry, and I can come back over and paint. We need to discuss what color to paint your room," Mr. Clark said as he placed a hand on my shoulder.

"Oh, Mr. Clark, I still have paint left over from when I painted this room. It's out in the garage, so when you come back, I will have it up here for you. Thank you both so much. I really appreciate this."

"You are welcome, baby," Mr. Daniels said as he gave me a warm hug. His words made me flinch. His voice was like an older Miles, and it made me uncomfortable.

Vicki and walked them both outside and helped them load their things into both trucks and stood outside as they drove off.

At that point, Phillip drove up, and my throat tightened. I slowly turned and headed for the front door, not realizing that Vicki wasn't following.

"What do you want, you son of a bitch?" Vicki said as Phillip got out of the car and walked to the edge of the driveway.

"Vicki, please. I just came over to speak to Maya," he said as he held his hands out, palms up.

"Maya has been hurt enough. Go home and leave her the hell alone. If she wanted to talk to you, she would call you," Vicki yelled at him as she balled up her fist and punched her leg with every syllable of every word she spoke to him.

When I saw my cousin walk slowly to him, I sprinted back down the driveway to her. I knew her so well and knew that there would be no more words. She would hit him.

I grabbed her and, as I cut my eyes at him, tried to drag her toward the house.

Phillip lunged toward me and grabbed my arm. The shock of his touch threw me off balance, and I tripped and fell hard on to the driveway. That was enough ammunition to spark my cousin to jump him. Before I could get up or say anything to her, she lunged toward him and slapped him hard, not once but twice. I heard the pop of each one, and I felt the sting as I watched him flinch and stand there and take her abuse.

It felt as if the earth had started running in slow motion because I couldn't believe that she had slapped him, and I didn't think he could believe it either because he stepped back and grabbed his face. He looked hurt and just stood, holding his face with his mouth open for a few seconds, before he turned and walked away.

I sat on the driveway and watched him until he drove out of sight. I turned and looked toward my cousin, who was just standing a few feet in front of me, not moving, her back to me.

"Vicki?"

She slowly turned and walked toward me. Her eyes looked wild, and her beautiful, curly hair had slipped out of the bun on top of her head and was hanging wildly around her face. She had tears in her eyes, and one slipped and fell down her cheek as she reached down for my hand, and I grabbed it and allowed her to pull me up.

I hugged her. We hugged each other for a long time. No words were spoken as we released our embrace and walked toward and into my house.

We sat on the couch in silence, holding hands, until she spoke, stirring the air with her words.

"I can feel your pain. I don't want you to hurt," she whispered as she turned to meet my eyes.

"I don't know what to say. I am hurting. But I'm more so numb than anything. So much has happened in such a short time. It's almost like I'm not supposed to be happy. I don't know what to do or how to feel anymore. I'm hurt and scared because I don't know where Daren is or if he intends to hurt me," I said through tears and sobbing hiccups.

Vicki released my hand and put her arm around my shoulder. I laid my head on her shoulder and cried.

After what seemed like forever, I finally calmed down.

"Vicki, I let Phillip in last night so that he could say what he had to say. I wanted to put a stop to the calls and the impromptu visits. I thought that maybe he would just leave me alone after that. I told him that I would put an order of protection on him if he came back. I'm beginning to wonder if I should."

"If that's what you want, Maya, but honestly, I don't think you will hear from him anymore."

"Okay. I will take your word for it." I decided to call him just to reiterate what I had said the night before.

He picked up on the first ring. "Maya?"

"Phillip, I meant what I said last night. Today was a freebie. But don't ever come to my house or call me again."

"Maya, I'm so sorry. I know there is no explaining this. I never meant to hurt you. I just don't know what to say other than I'm sorry.

Please, baby. Please don't throw us away. Let me make this better. Let me spend the rest of my life making this up to you. Please," he said through sobs.

I was disgusted, and if I could have spit on him through the phone, then I would.

"I didn't want to be in a relationship from the beginning. But you kept pushing and pushing. I finally agreed to it, and you hurt me. You did something to me that I asked you not to do. You cheated on me because you are weak. You let what's in your pants drive you. And I cannot be with someone who is like that. Because if you cheated on me once, you will do it again, and I can't let you continue to play with my heart like that."

"Maya, I love you. Please don't do this to me," he said through sobs.

"I'm telling you, Phillip, that I don't want to see you again as long as I live. We are done. Go and find Kiera. Hell, I don't care what you do as long as you go away and never come back," I said as my lip quivered, and tears spilled down my face. I felt as if my throat had something stuck in it, and I couldn't breathe. I took a very ragged breath. I closed my eyes and tried to get myself together.

I could hear him sniffling. I knew he was crying, and I didn't care. "I love you, Maya. I love you so much."

My eyes snapped open. I could feel so much anger in me for him. "Phillip, you don't love me. If you did, we would not be here, in this moment, saying goodbye."

I didn't want to listen to his sobbing anymore, and I quietly hung up. I slid down to my knees and into a praying position over the couch. Vicki slid to the floor with me.

Vicki put her hand on my back and rubbed it as I tried to get it together. I prayed long and hard for healing.

I got up from my knees then walked upstairs to my bedroom. They had put my room back together and cleaned it. Only thing needed was some paint. They hung the curtains back up so I was able to shower and climb into bed.

CHAPTER 12

Sleeping All Day

I woke to the smell of food and the grumbling of my stomach. I didn't have the energy to get up, so I rolled over to my stomach and pushed my hair back off my face. Opening my eyes, I glanced at the clock. It read 12:17 p.m. Groaning, I rolled on to my side and pulled the covers over my head.

I heard my door creak open and footsteps toward the bed.

"Maya, I fixed you some breakfast. You have to eat." Pulling the covers from my head, I looked up at my cousin. She was holding a tray full of food. I smiled as my stomach growled at the smells and buffet she fixed me.

I quickly sat up so that she could put the tray down.

"I will be back. I'm going to get my food so that we can eat together."

I looked down at the jam-packed tray. Waffles with fresh strawberries and warm syrup sat on the tray. Bacon, ham, and sausage were to the side. The sight of all three made me smile. There were shrimp and grits with scrambled eggs and cheese together in a bowl. And last but not least, a big mug of fresh chicory coffee. I smiled as I reached down for that and took a sip. The strength and bold flavor woke me up and cleared the cobwebs from my head in an instant.

I looked up as Vicki walked in with a tray filled with the same food and coffee as my tray. She got in the bed next to me. After she got comfortable, we looked at each other, then bowed our heads to pray. She reached over and turned the TV on and quickly found a movie. We sat and ate in silence as we watched an action-packed movie. About thirty minutes later, my plate was clean, and so was Vicki's. We both got up at the same time and placed our trays on the floor then got back in the bed and got comfortable as we continued watching the movie.

My phone rang and jolted me away. It was an unlisted number. I frowned as I said hello.

"Hello?" There was no response, but I could hear breathing on the other end, then silence as they hung up.

"Who was that?"

"I don't know. But I got a strange feeling that it was Daren," I said as chills ran up my back.

We both looked at each other. Nothing else was said as we both tried to get back into the movie.

"Well, cousin. I'm going home. Derrick has been calling me since last night. But call me if you need me. I love you," Vicki said as she rose from the bed and started getting the trays together to take downstairs.

I got up to help, and we walked downstairs together. "I will be fine, Vicki, no worries. Go spend time with your boo. I love you too."

After we worked together to load the dishwasher and get the kitchen back in order, Vicki left. I felt alone, and I stood at the window, with my arms wrapped around my body.

My phone rang again, and I ran to get it after I alarmed the house.

It was the same unlisted number. Again, breathing on the other end, some noise in the background that sounded like cars driving by. Then they hung up.

I was frightened, but there was no one to call to help.

Climbing back into my bed, I sat and watched TV until I fell asleep, waking with a jolt to the phone ringing again.

This time, I had more to say to the person on the other end of the phone. "Hello! Who is this, and why do you keep calling and hanging up?"

The breathing gave to a low chuckle. "You miss me, Maya? Well, I miss you. I miss the way you let me touch you. I miss the taste of you, the smell of you, and the feel of you. I will have you again. You are going to give it to me, or I will take it. Make it easy on yourself." He chuckled again then hung up.

I sat, sobbing, holding my phone. "Please, God, help me" was all I could say out loud.

I was wondering when Daren would pop up again. The sound of his voice held so much anger. I was so sick to my stomach. I was scared, and my whole body trembled as I sat and cried. I couldn't help but wonder if he was near. I was wondering if somehow, someway, he could see through the walls of my house and into my room where I sat. I knew that was ridiculous, but I was scared, and all sorts of crazy thoughts were running through my mind. I didn't know what to do. Frantically, I looked around the room.

Jumping up, I ran and looked out of all windows in the house. I ran downstairs and checked the windows and the doors. Even though I had set it earlier, I checked to make sure the alarm was set.

I flipped on the porch light and ran back upstairs to get into the safety of my bed. I was scared, and my body was shaking. I laid there and cried. My phone rang, and I jumped. My heart was beating so fast. I looked at the caller ID, and it was Mr. Clark's number.

Clearing my throat and quickly taking a sip of water, I answered the call. "Hello."

"Hey, baby girl. Is it okay to come over and paint? It will only take about an hour two hours tops."

"Oh yes, sir, that sounds good. Come right on over." I closed my eyes. If only for two hours, I would feel safe.

"Okay, I will be there in about twenty minutes," he said then hung up.

I got up and made the bed, put some clothes on and tamed my hair, washed my face, and brushed my teeth. By the time I was done, the doorbell rang. I cringed, wondering if it was Mr. Clark or Daren. My heart began to beat fast as I slowly walked down the steps and to the window to look out.

I closed my eyes and exhaled as I disarmed the house and let him in.

He gave me a big hug and squeeze as he walked past me and into the house.

"Do you need any help, Mr. Clark?"

"Oh, no, Maya, thanks. No help needed at all. Go ahead and relax," he said as he headed for the stairs, with all his paint gear in tow.

Walking into the living room, I turned on the TV then sat Indian style on the sofa. I couldn't focus on what was on, so I just sat, eyes out of focus to the point where they crossed. I blinked a couple of times to focus then looked down at the floor.

Reaching over the arm of the sofa, I grabbed the phone and dialed Vicki's number.

"Hey, Maya, you okay?"

I broke down, crying, at her voice and was trying to tell her what happened, but I knew she couldn't understand me because I couldn't understand myself.

"Maya, what's wrong? Please slow down, take a breath, and calm down. Tell me what's wrong."

"Maya." The sound of Mr. Clark's soft voice startled me, and I jumped, dropping the phone in my lap.

His face held concern.

I could hear Vicki yelling my name over and over on the phone. I picked the phone out of my lap and held it in my hand as I stared at Mr. Clark. I pleaded for help with my eyes.

Mr. Clark leaned over and took the phone from my hand. He smelled of paint and had spots of it on his clothes, arms, face, and hair. He patted my shoulder.

"Hello," Mr. Clark's deep voice sounded into the phone. "Oh, hello, Vicki. How are you? I don't know what's wrong. I was upstairs painting, and I heard her crying. I came down as fast as I could. She is just sitting here, crying. Yes, I think you and Derrick should come on by. Okay, I will be here with her until you get here. Okay, bye."

Mr. Clark placed the phone on the cradle and put his hand on my back and rubbed. I exhaled at his touch, put my head down, and cried hard. I cried so hard my body shook. Mr. Clark just kept rubbing my back. My crying slowed, and my breathing evened out. I just sat and rocked, staring off. I was scared.

The doorbell rang, and Mr. Clark turned to go answer the door. With his hand no longer on my back, I started to cry uncontrollably again. My body rocked as I sobbed into my hands.

Vicki sat on the couch next to me and pulled me to her. I leaned my head on her shoulder. All I could see was Derrick's feet as he stood on the other side of me. Mr. Clark had his heavy hand on my back again. I closed my eyes and tried to calm myself.

After what seemed like an hour, I heard Vicki's voice. "Maya, what happened?"

Sitting up, I glanced at Derrick then into the eyes of my cousin. "Daren called me."

"What!" they all said at once.

Derrick sat in the chair across from me. Mr. Clark went and sat in the other chair, facing Derrick.

Derrick spoke first. "Maya, what did he say to have you so broken like this?"

"He told me that he misses me, and said that he would have me again. Told me that if I don't, he would take it. I'm so scared, and I don't know what to do. I don't feel safe." I started squeezing my hands together and rocking.

"I can't believe my brother. I really don't know what's wrong with him. I'm so tired of all the pain that he brings to people. Dad, what are we going to do about this?"

"Well, son, I don't know. I need to tell your mom what's going on. But I really don't know what we need to do."

I looked to my cousin. She was crying and started rubbing her hand in my hair and down my face.

"Well, let me see if I can get this idiot on the phone," Derrick said has he pulled his phone out and started dialing.

My heart started beating fast. I felt out of control and scared at the thought of him calling his brother. I put my head down in my hands and waited.

Derrick hit the speaker, and I could hear the phone ringing. After about three rings, I could hear a click and Daren's voice.

"Man, why do you keep calling me? If it's not you, it's Dad. Both of you need to leave me the hell alone."

I stopped breathing and raised my head from my hands. His voice was like nails on a chalkboard. I was scared. There was so much anger in that tone. I didn't ever remember him being that way.

"Daren, why are you harassing Maya? Why don't you just leave her alone? She has gone through enough! Don't you think that you need some help?"

"Derrick, go to hell. I don't need any help! She is going to need some help when I'm done with her!" he said, letting out a loud, frightening laugh.

"Son, why are you doing this?" Mr. Clark's tone was stern. I heard no love in his deep voice.

"Dad?" His voice was shaky.

"Yes, son. It's me. Why are you doing this to her, taking her through all this pain?"

"Dad, I love her. I've loved her since we were young. But all she wants is for us to be friends. I can't live with that."

"So you just want to force her to be with you? Son, if that's all she wants, then you should have just given her that. You can't make someone be with you. Now look at the mess you have created. You vandalized her home, and now you are calling her, threatening her. Do you think she wants anything to do with you now? Whatever friendship you could have had is no longer salvageable. You are hurting her, and it's not right. Leave this young lady alone. Your mom and I raised you better than this. We didn't raise you to be this person that you are right now. Wherever you are, just come to me and your mom's house. We are here for you, son."

I heard Daren sobbing on the phone. "Dad, I'm sorry." Then the phone clicked, and there was silence. He had hung up.

I looked at Mr. Clark. He closed his eyes and rubbed his hands across his face. He had been crying. I turned and glanced at Derrick. Tears were sliding down his face. I felt no comfort in either, and that made me more scared than ever.

Glancing over at Vicki, I began to cry again. "Vicki, I don't know what to do. I'm so scared. I'm so scared."

"Maya, I think you should go away for a while. Give Derrick, my wife, and I some time to try and find Daren before something bad happens. We love you, and we don't want Daren to harm you. We want you safe."

"I think that's a good idea, Maya. Vicki, I think you should go with her. Get her out of town. You both should leave soon." Derrick pulled Vicki up to him in an embrace and kissed her gently on the lips. She hugged him tight.

I felt nothing but sadness. So many times, I'd tried to find that type of love, and love continued to fail me. I was alone, running from a man that I thought was my friend, hurting because I thought Phillip was the one; and he turned out to be just like all other men, a liar and a cheater. I felt my heart hardening, and I felt a strength come from nowhere.

I reached over and picked up my phone and dialed the number to Continental Airlines. As I was waiting for the phone to connect, I turned and glanced at my cousin, who was still in an embrace with Derrick.

"I'm going to Atlanta, Vicki. You don't have to go with me, but I welcome the company."

"Maya, I'm going with you," she said, breaking away from Derrick.

I made reservations for two on a flight that was leaving the next morning at 8:15. Derrick took Vicki home so that she could pack. Mr. Clark hugged me and kissed me on the cheek and made me promise to keep in touch then he left.

I quickly packed then took a shower and washed my hair and pulled it into a tight bun on the top of my hair. I applied very little makeup, only enough to hide the dark marks under my eyes and the red, splotchy skin.

I needed to go to my office and pick up my laptop. I went through the house and checked all windows and doors to make sure they were locked. I alarmed the house as I walked to the garage entrance.

I was downtown within twenty minutes. I sprinted to the elevator after parking my car in the visitor spots, which were closer to the building. Once in my office, I quickly packed my laptop bag, headset, and sprinted back to the elevator bank.

I was back in my car and on the freeway, headed home. I needed to pack for my trip to Atlanta and try to get some rest for the flight. I couldn't think about Daren. I had to push that out of my mind and trust that Derrick and Mr. Clark would handle this issue.

Hitting the button on my garage-door opener, I eased my car into the garage. After turning off the car ignition, I hit the button to close the garage door. Once I knew it was down and secure, I exited my car, grabbed my laptop bag and purse, and headed for the entry to my safe space. Doing anything outside my home put me in the center of stressful situations with stressful people—people who cared nothing about me, my heart, or my feelings.

Walking into my home, I closed my eyes and exhaled. My home, my sanctuary, my peace. I hoped Derrick and Mr. Clark would be able to take care of this issue quickly so that I could return to my place of peace. Once I returned home, I was not going to do anything but go to work and come home. If need be, I could have my groceries delivered.

I opened the door and heard the *beep, beep, beep* of the door as I walked in. I was so deep in thought its sound didn't register. Closing the door, I engaged both locks then reached to the side and engaged the alarm. I turned around with my back to the door.

Standing in front of the door, I felt nothing but defeat. I just wanted to stand and listen to the beautiful quiet of my home.

I just stood and quieted my breathing, eyes closed, still holding on to my laptop bag and purse.

My eyes flew open. What was that? I didn't feel alone. My heart started racing. Something moved and sliced the quietness. Someone was in my sanctuary. I stepped forward and set my things down on the side table.

I stood and listened. I was listening for the direction of that movement that interrupted my comfortable silence. It was hard for me to hear anything but my loud beating heart and my now-ragged breaths. My eyes widened. I was trying to see anything moving in the house. It was hard to see anything but shadows cast by the streetlights coming through the window. Everything had a shadow; every shadow was suspect.

In and out, in and out, *thump-thump, thump-thump.* I couldn't hear past that. I had to gain control of my breathing. I focused on steadying my breathing. Deep breaths in and out. Finally, the hard thumping of my heart and the ragged breaths slowed down.

At this point, I couldn't turn around and walk back out the door. Whoever was in my house knew that I was here. They heard the *beep, beep, beep* of the door when I walked in. Wait. Oh god. When I walked in, I didn't disarm the house. It was already disarmed. That someone in my house knew the code and disarmed the alarm.

My gun. Shit. It was upstairs in my nightstand. I started moving toward the direction of the stairway. When I made it to the foyer, I stopped and listened. I couldn't hear anything, so I continued walking toward the stairway. If I could just make it to my room, I could get my gun. My gun would make me feel safer.

My breathing sped up again, and the loud thumping of my heart made me dizzy. I made it to the stair rail and leaned on it, trying to get steady. Closing my eyes, I inhaled and exhaled, trying to let it pass. When I could feel my breathing slowing down and the dizziness subside, I opened my eyes.

I saw movement to my right in the kitchen, and I sucked in a breath. In my head, I heard, *Run!* And that's what I did. I tried to take two steps at a time to get me there quicker. I heard footsteps of someone running, hard shoes on the smooth surface of my hardwood floors.

Halfway up the stairs, I felt a hand on my foot, and I was yanked down. I lost my balance and went down to my knee as I was pulled toward the intruder.

I screamed, "No!" and I used all the strength that I could muster to kick back, using my free leg. I was trying to connect with anything to bring pain, something that would give me time to get to my gun.

I heard a grunt, and my foot was released. I scrambled up the stairs using hands and feet, hoping I would get to the top quicker.

I made it to the landing, and I heard hard stomps coming up the stairs behind me. I stood and ran as fast as I could toward my room and the direction of my nightstand. But the faster I ran, the farther away my nightstand seemed.

I felt hands grab me, and I felt myself go airborne as I was slammed to the ground.

"Ugh!" I grunted, feeling pain in my left side, where I landed.

The wind was knocked out of me, and I moaned, rocking back and forth, trying to get my bearings, and waited for the pain to subside. My shoulder was the location of excruciating pain. I was almost certain it was out of the socket. I had to get it back together. I quickly sat up and slammed my body down on the arm to pop it back in place.

"Ahh!" I screamed, feeling it slip back into place.

Lifting my head from the floor, I looked up to where that person was standing. The intruder grabbed a handful of my hair and yanked me up to my feet.

I screamed and started flailing my arms, trying to hit this person. My swings were out of control, and I was only connecting with air.

I adjusted my stance, and I kicked toward the intruder. I connected with something soft. I heard a grunt.

"Shit! Bitch, I will kill you if you do that again!"

I stood still. That voice was unmistakable. I didn't need to see his face. I knew exactly who he was. At that point, my heart dropped, and I feared for my life. I wasn't ready to die. I took a step back and looked around frantically for a way past him. He was busy trying to rub away the pain I inflicted to his nuts.

I stepped to the right, and he straitened up and stepped in front of me. "Don't you move, stupid bitch, or I will end your life where you stand." His hands were still below, trying to help him recover.

"Daren, why are you here? Why are you in my house? Why are you doing this to me?"

"Daren, why are you here? Why are you in BLAH, BLAH, BLAH! Shut up!" he spat, mocking me with a high-pitched voice.

"I told your stupid ass. If I can't have you, no one else will. I've been following your simple ass everywhere. For six months, I've watched you and that piece of shit! I was pissed. I've had so many opportunities to kill you both, but I waited. I hoped your relationship would end quickly. When it finally ended, I was so happy. I knew Phillip and that whore were fucking. I've always known this information. In my mind, I wanted to swoop in and save the day and rescue your broken heart. But, of course, I fucked that up when I attacked you at your party. I should have been more patient. But that's neither here nor there. Here I am. Here we are."

He reached up and grabbed the back of my head and slammed me into something hard, something cold, and something that shattered when my face hit it. I moaned and started crying. I fell to my knees. I tasted and smelled blood. Reaching up to touch my face, I felt blood and sharp pieces of glass sticking out of my skin. The room started to spin. No, now wasn't the time for dizzy. I could feel myself leaning over, then nothing but darkness.

I didn't know how long I was out, but when I woke, I had almost forgotten what transpired. The room was no longer dark. It was bright with the lights from the lamps he had turned on. I blinked, trying to focus as I looked around the room. I realized that I was laying on my bed in my bra and panties. I started crying. I closed my eyes as my sobs rocked my body.

"Please, God, help me."

I felt the bed move, and I sucked in a breath as I opened my eyes and look up at him. He had this smile on his face. He was so amused by my pain, my tears, and the fact that I was at his mercy. I tried to roll away from him, and I couldn't. Looking toward my arm, I noticed that it was tied to the bed by a rope, the same for my other arm and both legs. They were tied tight, preventing me from barely moving.

"Daren, untie me. Let me go! Why are you doing this?" I sobbed uncontrollably.

My pleas were on deaf ears. He could care less. He leaned down closer to my face. I started trying to move away from him again. No luck. This ugly evil laugh burst from him. Grabbing my face with both hands, pushing glass deeper in my face, caused me to scream out in pain.

His eyes were crazy. I could smell alcohol on his breath, and the smell turned my stomach. He let my face go and stood.

I couldn't stop crying. So many what-ifs were in my mind as I watched this maniac begin to take off his clothing.

Realization hit me. "No, oh no, please, Daren. Don't do this please."

He laughed. "Oh, Maya baby. You don't have a choice. I'm going to shower, then I'm coming back to take what should have been mine. Then I'm going to kill you."

I sucked in a breath. *Oh god. I'm not ready. Please, someone, help me.*

The phone rang, stopping him in his tracks. He turned and walk back toward the nightstand and snatched the phone off its cradle. He laughed as he looked at the caller ID.

"Your stupid cousin," he spat as he turned and threw the phone against the wall, breaking it.

He turned and walked toward the bathroom. I watched him go straight to the linen closet, open the door, and retrieve towels. When did he get so familiar with my house? Daren had never gone past the downstairs area, or so I thought. He opened the shower door and turned on the water, stepping in when he was satisfied.

I didn't have much time. I had to get my thoughts together. Turning my head, I took a good look at the rope that had my hand bound to the bed. They were tight, but there was one issue. He had the rope tied so that the end was in my hand. I took my fingers and worked it through until I felt it loosen. I was able to slide my hand free. I turned to see what he was doing. His back was to me, and he was soaping up his hair. I rolled to the left and untied my left hand, making sure to keep my eyes on him as much as possible. I sat up and untied both legs then scooted over to the edge of the bed, placing my feet on the floor. My T-shirt was on the floor, so I reached down to grab it.

Looking to my left, I checked to see if Daren had turned around. His back was still to me. I reached for the nightstand drawer and opened it in search of my gun. The spot that always occupied my gun was empty.

"Shit," I whispered.

Jumping up, I glanced toward the shower and made my way to the door. He was rinsing his body, and our eyes met. I took off running, and I listened for him. I heard the shower door open, and a loud bang, and the shattering of the glass. I made it to the landing at the top of the stairs and started down. I was running for dear life.

"Bitch, how did you get loose?" I heard him scream down the stairs.

I turned my head as my bare feet connected with the wood floor at the bottom of the steps. I quickly glanced back to see where he was and what I had time to do. He was stomping down the stairs, fully naked. He was halfway to me. I decided to go through the garage door. My keys were on the table next to the door, easy access. But I didn't make it far. He tackled me, and the weight of his body made me lose balance, and I crashed to the floor. His heavy body weighed me down, preventing me from recovering. I screamed and tried to buck him from my back. He was just too heavy and too strong for me to get him off me.

He wrapped his left hand around my neck. I grunted and tried to use my elbows to hit him in the side. That did nothing but make me tired. My tiny body didn't do any damage to him.

I could feel the full weight of his body as he took his right hand and yanked at my underwear.

"No! Daren, no!" I yelled and used all my energy to shake him off me.

I whimpered as his left hand tightened around my neck. I knew what was about to happen. I felt so powerless. I wished that I could die in that moment so that I would not endure the damage he was about to do to me.

He succeeded at ripping my underwear from me enough to allow him access.

"I've been waiting to get back between these thighs. I hoped it would be while in a relationship with you. But, hey, this will do. You fighting me is doing nothing but turn me on. Keep fighting, baby."

"You are fucking crazy!" In my mind, that was what I said, but because of the hold he had on my neck, my words failed me.

He took his knee and pushed my legs apart. I tried to squeeze them shut, but his body had fallen between them, and I couldn't prevent what was about to happen. I cried and tried to steady my breathing. The more I moved, the tighter his hand got. The weight of him on my body and his hand around my neck was making me feel like I wanted to pass out. *Please, God, help me.*

I felt him at my opening, then I felt him forcefully enter me. I tried to scream, but no sound came out. He started moving slowly at first, then he sped up. When he pushed in, his hand got tighter around my neck as he pulled down. When he pulled out, his hand wasn't so tight.

"Oh, yes, Maya. This is mine! You are mine!" He grunted as he took what did not belong to him.

His speed slowed down, and his hand started squeezing tighter around my neck. Too tight. Oh god. I couldn't breathe. Then there was the welcomed darkness.

When I regained consciousness, I was on my back. Daren was on top of me. His hand was around my neck.

"No, please stop!"

He started squeezing my neck tighter. I tried to hit him, and he paused long enough to grab both hands and pin them above my head. He leaned down and tried to kiss me, but I turned my head. He started to lick on my neck then down to my breasts and latched onto my nipple. I felt so sick to my stomach.

I closed my eyes and tried to think of happy times. I thought about my mom and dad who had been living their best life, traveling the world. I missed them so much and couldn't wait until they returned from their year-long trip.

My thoughts were interrupted when my cell phone rang from my purse on the table next to the garage door. When that stopped ringing, my house phone began to ring again. Back and forth from phone to phone. The ringing never fazed him. *Please, whoever is trying to call me, come save me.*

"Maya, oh shit, this is good." He started licking on my nipples again. "Maya, tell me you love me."

I didn't respond. I just laid there, unmoving, hoping for him to get off me and go ahead and kill me. How could I live in this world after this?

"I said, tell me you love me!" he yelled, pumping harder in and out. "Oh, no response? I got something for you, bitch."

He lifted his head to my left shoulder and bit down hard. He bit so hard I swore I heard a pop. I scream so loud and for so long. The pain in my arm fueled my screams.

I heard a noise sounding like the door opening, and the alarm dinged and prompted for it to be disarmed.

"Maya!" I heard the screams of both Derrick and Vicki.

Daren stopped pumping, and I felt him pull out of me. He jumped up and took off toward the stairway, then up the stairs. "Shit!" he screamed before the bedroom door slammed shut.

"Thank you, God," I whispered as I rolled over on my side and found darkness again.

I woke to beeping, brightness, and a coldness. Was I dead?

"Maya?" I felt movement to my left and a squeeze to my hand. I turned and looked into the eyes of my cousin. Her eyes were puffy, and her face was red. She had tears running down her face.

"Vicki?" I tried to sit up then noticed where I was. I was in a hospital. "What happened?" As awareness of what happened to me hit, I panicked. "Please tell me Daren is locked up."

Vicki started sobbing and released my hand. "Maya, he was gone by the time the police arrived. He came flying down the stairs fully dressed and barreled into Derrick. Derrick fell and hit his head. He is down the hall because he hasn't gained consciousness."

"No! Oh no!" I started screaming, and the beeps got faster.

The nurse ran in, and I could see her putting something into my IV bag. "No!" After a minute, I started feeling tired, and I closed my eyes. I welcomed the darkness that seemed to be my safe place.

When I woke again and my eyes adjusted, I could see that it was daylight outside. Vicki's head was down on the bed, and I could hear soft snores coming from her. She was holding my hand, but since she was asleep, it was a loose grip.

I tried stretching my body and started feeling pains. My vagina was so sore, my thighs were hurting, and my shoulder where he bit me was on fire. I reached up to my face and was met with bandages.

"Oh my god."

My words woke Vicki.

"Cousin, you're awake. How are you feeling?" my cousin croaked in her just-woke-up voice.

I started crying. "Vicki, I wish he would have done what he said."

"Done what, Maya?"

"He said he was going to take what was his, and he was going to kill me. I can't live anymore after this."

I could feel her squeeze my hand. She started crying. "Maya, no! We are going to get through this. As soon as you are released, we are going to Atlanta like we planned. The doctor said he would release you this morning and will let us know at that time if you are cleared to travel. Do not give up because of an idiot! I love you, Maya. You are going to be okay. You got me, girl?"

I shook my head yes and relaxed. At that moment, the nurse entered the room with a tall man with a stethoscope hanging from his neck. I assumed he was the doctor.

He smiled. I did not. "Ms. Fontenot. I am Dr. Frank. How are you feeling?"

I cleared my throat. "I'm sore, some pain, but I'm okay, I guess."

"We checked you out, ran some STD tests. Everything was negative. Nurse Sharon here is going to give you something called the morning-after pill. I am releasing you to your cousin." He turned toward Vicki. "She is cleared to fly. She should have no problems traveling." He turned back to me. "I want you to come see me in a month. I want to take a look at your shoulder. We had to give you nine stitches. Keep your shoulder clean and dry and in the sling Nurse Sharon is going to help you with. We had to remove several pieces of glass from the right side of your face and forehead. You are lucky it missed your eye. Some of those were not as deep. There are three places on your face that need more care. Keep your wounds clean. The three that are covered now need to be covered until they are no longer bleeding. Take it easy for the next six weeks. Nurse Sharon is going to give you some paperwork for your job and some prescriptions for pain. You need to rest so that you can heal. Do you have any questions for me?"

I shook my head. "No."

"Okay, Ms. Fontenot. If you feel like your wounds are not healing, please call me, okay?"

"Okay."

"Take care, Ms. Fontenot."

"Thank you."

I inhaled and exhaled as Nurse Sharon walked toward me. She worked on removing the IV and bandaging it. On the table, she picked up a cup with a pill in it. She handed me to pill, along with a cup of water.

"Ms. Fontenot, you may feel some cramping later, but it's just the pill working. Okay?"

"Okay."

"Go ahead and get dressed, and I will help you with the sling for your arm. Do you need me to help you?"

"Oh, no, ma'am. My cousin can help me."

"Okay, I will leave you to it. I will be back shortly."

When she exited the room and closed the door, I sat up and, with the help of Vicki, got dressed. As promised, Nurse Sharon came in and gently put the sling on my arm and adjusted it so that it was comfortable.

"Okay, Ms. Fontenot. You must be in this sling at all times except for when you shower. There are bandages on your shoulder that are okay if they get wet. Just pat them dry after you get out of the shower. Do not remove the bandages. We will remove them and the stitches when you come back to see us. Any questions?"

"No, ma'am. Thank you."

"Okay, honey. Take care of yourself."

"Yes, ma'am. Thank you. I will." I tried not to cry as Nurse Sharon leaned down to give me a gentle hug.

Vicki helped me stand.

"Vicki, I want to see Derrick."

"Okay," she whispered as tears welled up in her eyes.

He was four doors down the hall. When we walked in the room, I noticed Mr. Clark on the left side, holding Derrick's right hand, and Mrs. Clark on the right side, holding his left hand. They both looked up as we walked into the room.

"Oh baby, we are so sorry," Mrs. Clark said as she got up and rushed toward me. She rubbed her hand on my back as she tried to lean in for a hug. It was awkward.

"Maya baby, I'm trying not to hug you and cause you any pain." She let out a nervous laugh, but a smile never made it to her mouth. Her eyes held so much sadness, and she appeared to be very tired.

"Thank you, Mrs. Clark. I'm okay," I said, and leaned as far as I could to give her a hug.

"Maya, how are you feeling?" Mr. Clark said as he walked toward me and lightly touched the side of my head. He put his arm around my back to hug me and to avoid hurting me.

"I'm sore and in some pain, Mr. Clark, but I'm alive," I said, trying not to cry.

I turned from his tired but kind eyes and walked toward Derrick's bed. He just looked as if he was sleeping. "How is he? What are the doctors saying?"

Mr. Clark spoke first. "Well, the doctors are saying that he is doing good. The swelling on his brain has gone down fast. His vital signs have all returned to normal. Now all we can do is wait on him to wake up." I heard him let out a quick breath, and I turned to look at him.

Vicki had pulled a chair to the end of the bed, and her hand was on Derrick's foot, her head down on the bed.

I heard a sigh, and my eyes went wide. It sounded like it came from Derrick. My head whipped around to look at his face. His eyes were open and on Vicki, but, of course, she didn't know.

"Mm," came from his mouth, and the beeps on the machine sped up.

All of us gasped in unison as we peered into his face. Mr. Clark squeezed past me and pushed the button on Derrick's bed to call for the nurse.

"Calm down, baby," came the shaky voice from Mrs. Clark. She had walked behind and past Vicki to regain her position next to him. She placed a hand on his shoulder and rubbed it. She closed her eyes, lips moving, and every few seconds, I heard, "Thank you, Father."

The beeping from the machine started to slow down, and his panicked breaths began to level out. He closed his eyes and appeared to relax.

The nurse burst into the room, followed by a tall man with a stethoscope wrapped around his neck. I assumed from his look that he was the doctor.

"Mr. Clark, I'm Dr. Rush. Nurse Jess is going to remove the intubation tube from your throat. She will give you instructions on what she needs you to do."

Derrick's eyes were wide, and it appeared he was about to start panicking again. The beeps started speeding up.

"Baby, relax so the nurse can tend to you," came the sweet voice of Mrs. Clark.

Vicki stood and moved away from the bed to give the doctor and nurse room to access Derrick. I slowly made my way to her side and held her hand.

Within a half hour, the nurse had removed the tube, poked and prodded, and she quickly exited the room.

The doctor turned and looked from face to face before he began to speak. "Mr. Clark appears to be well and is positively responding to stimuli. I want to keep him through the night for observation, and I will return in the morning to discuss my thoughts on his release. Everyone, have a good night." The doctor walked toward the door where Vicki and I stood. We separated to give him access to leave.

After the doctor left, we all moved closer to Derrick's bed. He smiled, cleared his throat, closed and opened his eyes, and focused them on Vicki. "Hello." His voice was rough.

"Rest, baby," came the voice of Mrs. Clark.

She grabbed the cup of water and angled the straw to his mouth. He sipped the water until the cup was empty. Mrs. Clark refilled the water and moved it toward his mouth. This time, he only drank half the cup and angled his head away so that the straw was away from his mouth. He cleared his throat and smiled again.

"Everyone looks so serious. I'm okay." His voice sounded better, but still a little rough.

We all laughed.

His face quickly got serious when his eyes landed on me. He cleared his throat again. His voice was a bit raspy. "Maya, how are you?"

Tears started rolling down my face, and I didn't know when I had started to cry. I smiled and quickly wiped the tears from my face. "I'm okay." My voice came out in a whisper.

"Dad, where is Daren?" Derrick said when his eyes focused on his father.

"Well, son, when the police arrived, Daren was long gone. The window in Maya's bedroom was open, and the area below appeared to be where he landed. So the thought was that he jumped from the window and ran. The police went to his house, and he wasn't there either. He is on the run. An arrest warrant has been issued for him."

Derrick sighed, shook his head, and ran a hand across his face.

My heart sank as the realization finally hit me hard. Everything that had happened to me and Derrick was all my fault. A moment of weakness had almost cost us our lives.

"I'm sorry." My voice was low but loud enough for everyone in the room to hear me. I knew they heard me because everyone turned to look at me. I could feel my body start to shake.

I could feel my cousin's hand around my waist as she pulled me closer to her.

"Maya, no matter what happened between you and Daren, none of this is your fault. It is not okay to hurt someone because they don't want you. This wasn't right! He hurt you and Derrick. He raped you, beat you, and bit chunks from your body. He hit Derrick so hard that he had swelling on his brain. This was not your fault!"

My cousin was starting to lose her composure. I couldn't help her because I was losing mine as well. The more she talked, the more that lump in my throat hurt. My hand was now over my mouth. I was trying to refrain from screaming. I was trying to hold in my sobs. I was trying to keep any kind of sound from escaping from my mouth.

Vicki walked away from me so that she could lean against the wall.

"Baby, are you okay? Come over and sit next to me on the bed."

Vicki walked over and sat at the foot of the bed and laid across Derrick's legs. He pushed the button on his bed so that the bed would adjust and put him closer to her. He ran his hand through her now-unruly curls. He laid his head back and closed his eyes.

Mrs. Clark walked toward me and laid a hand on the uninjured part of my back. "Maya baby, this is just a season. It didn't kill you. Daren didn't kill you, but you will be stronger. Hold your head up. You have a support system. We are here for you. Have you called your parents? I know they are taking their trip around the world, but maybe they need to know."

"No, ma'am. I don't want to interrupt their vacation. I don't want them to know yet."

"Okay, Maya. But I don't want you in that house by yourself until they find Daren."

"I think you and Vicki need to go ahead and go to Atlanta like you both planned. You need to call and change your reservations to give you both time to get home and finish packing." Derrick's voice was firm. He wasn't asking us; he was telling us.

"Vicki, all your clothes are still in my car. Take Maya home so she can pack. Both of you change your reservations. Baby, go now. I will feel better when you both are safe in Atlanta with your family."

Vicki sat up and stood from the bed. She moved closer to him and hugged him. I looked away while they shared their tender moment. I turned so that I could lay my head on Mrs. Clark's shoulder and put my arm around her back to give her an awkward hug.

Mr. Clark walked over to me and hugged me. "We love you, Maya. Call us so that we will know you and Vicki are okay."

"Yes, sir," I said as I broke the embrace and walked toward Derrick.

I could only pat his leg. I couldn't look in his face. I felt horrible. No matter how they tried to spin this, it was my fault.

CHAOS

Vicki and I were silent as we walked out of the hospital. Our silence continued the whole ride to my house. My stomach was uneasy the closer we got to my house.

Within an hour, we had changed our reservations, and my bags were packed.

I tried to not think about the things that had gone on in my house. I didn't know when or if I wanted to come back to this place of horror.

Vicki had called for an airport shuttle. Nothing was said as we loaded my bags into the back of the shuttle. We rode in silence to the airport. I sat with my head in my hand, deep in thought. I was looking forward to going to Atlanta to visit with my cousins. I had contacted my boss and explained the situation. I let her know that I wouldn't be in the office but would continue to work from my computer, and she agreed.

We arrived at the airport at 6:15, and we got out of the car and began unloading and checking in with the sky captain, who took our bags and tagged them and pointed us in the direction of our gate.

Vicki and I turned and walked toward security to check in then on to our gate.

After checking in, we found seats and sat and watched out the window at the planes coming and going.

"Vicki, I'm sorry for dragging you away from Derrick. You don't have to go with me," I said through tears.

"Maya, don't worry about it. There was no way that I would let you do this by yourself. I know you are hurting. So much has taken place in such a short time. I'm here for you for as long as you need me. And when you don't need me anymore, I will still be here."

"I wish I could go back to that day at the picnic and walk away from Daren. I should have never slept with him. I caused all this." I could feel my whole body shaking. I was breaking down again.

Vicki put her hand on my shoulder to calm me.

"Maya, this is not your fault. You did not know that Daren was so unstable. You didn't know what he was capable of. Everything will be okay. Derrick and his dad, or the cops, will find Daren and get him some help. Don't worry, and don't stress. You will just make yourself sick. So let's focus on visiting with our cousins and having some fun." She smiled, but tears fell from her eyes.

We both sat back and waited. I listened to the noise around me. Kids crying, laughter, and a couple behind me were arguing softly. I scanned the area suddenly, afraid that we were being watched. Chills came over my body, and I shivered. Something wasn't right. I sat forward and looked around. Daren was in that airport. I was sure of it.

CHAPTER 13

Getting Away

Vicki slept the whole flight. I sat and stared out the window as I drank glass after glass of rum and coke. Finally, the stewardess brought me a cup of coffee, said I needed that more than the rum. She smiled at me then walked away.

I reluctantly drank, and the coffee gave me a jolt. The caffeine had killed the little buzz that had begun to take over.

When the pilot announced our descent into Atlanta, I gently shook Vicki. She woke and smiled at me.

"Was I snoring?" She giggled and sat up.

I didn't smile. Just didn't have that in me. I couldn't shake the feeling that I had at the airport. I decided not to tell Vicki because I didn't want her as scared as I was.

"Nah, we are getting ready to land."

She smiled a weak smile then looked out the window.

After we landed and headed over to the baggage area, we went outside to wait for my cousins. Vicki called them once we got off the plane so that they would be on their way.

I began to look around. I had that same strange feeling that we were being watched. An airport full of people, and I didn't understand the feeling. I shivered and leaned my back against the wall next to the exit door.

"You okay, Maya? I can tell that something extra is on your mind. I see you keep looking around. What's going on?"

I didn't meet her eyes right away. I stared out into the night. The breeze whipped across my face, and I closed my eyes. I decided to tell her.

"Back at the airport in Houston, while we were waiting to board the plane, I got the strange feeling that we were being watched. I have that strange feeling here. Like Daren is watching us. I know that we are in a large airport with so many people around us, but I have this feeling of danger. Vicki, I'm scared. I know I keep saying this. But I really think he knows where I am."

Vicki looked away. I saw tears in her eyes, and her lip quivered. She reached into her purse and pulled out her phone. I knew who she was calling. She was calling Derrick.

She started sobbing softly into the phone, and I walked over to her and put my arm around her. I was the one in danger, not her, but I knew that she wasn't scared for herself; she was scared for me. She felt just as I did, and that was like I had no control over my own life.

She sobbed into the phone and told Derrick about what I said to her. She listened for a little, mumbled that she loved him too, and hung up. Her eyes met mine.

"Derrick said that his dad went by Daren's house and went inside. He had pictures of you all over the walls. Some he had written the word *bitch* all over. Some had knives in the center, and some he had torn in half and tacked to the wall. Daren wasn't there. There were signs of him being there. He said that they will keep trying to call him and drop by the house. They notified the detective that handled the last issue where Daren hurt that young woman so that he would know what was going on. He said he would try and locate Daren as well."

I couldn't respond to any of that. It didn't make me feel any better. All it did was tell me that he had to be here in Atlanta, and he was close by. The hairs on my neck were standing up, and a chill ran up my spine. I looked around frantically and backed back into the wall so that I wouldn't be so vulnerable.

"Maya, Vicki!" came the screams of familiar voices as a black SUV screeched to a halt at the curb.

I smiled as I realized who the voices came from. I walked over to the vehicle, with Vicki right behind me.

We all embraced and shed a few tears. Vicki and I piled in the back seat.

"Look, chicks, we are going out tonight, so I hope you heffas brought clothes for that!" This came from my loud cousin Tania.

"And even if they didn't bring any, we have something they can wear, I am so sure!" That came from my cousin Tasha.

We hadn't seen either of them in years, and it only seemed right that we came down here to get away and forget our troubles.

"Where are we staying? Neither one of you would let us book a hotel room!" Vicki yelled over the loud music.

"Aww, you both are staying with me," Tania yelled and laughed. "I know you don't want to stay with Tasha. Her house is nasty. She has visitors there that crawl around at night." She laughed long and hard at her joke.

"Cow, I know you didn't," Tasha said and laughed.

"You two should remember Tasha is not a clean one in the family!"

We all laughed. When the laughter died down, we all chatted back and forth, laughing and talking. Before we know it, we pulled up to the large, two-story home with a four-car garage. The SUV pulled into one of the garages.

"Wow, Tania, this is absolutely beautiful," I said in amazement. My cousin was doing well for herself, and I was proud of her.

Inside the house was even more beautiful. Tania showed us around, then we made our way upstairs, where she put us in rooms side by side, sharing a bathroom in the middle.

My room held a huge four-poster bed, sofa, love seat, and chair over in the corner next to a big-screen TV. The colors were brown and burgundy, with splashes of yellow and green everywhere. The artwork was beautiful and of flowers and trees, some of people. I looked around in amazement. I began to yawn. I didn't realize how tired I was.

"Girl, please, you won't be going to sleep tonight. At least not anytime soon! Relax, take a shower, a bath, or whatever, and come downstairs. We can eat and have some wine," Tania said as she headed back toward the door. She closed the door as she walked out.

I looked toward the restroom and headed toward it to check on Vicki.

"Hey, you okay?"

"Oh yeah, I'm good. It's good being here with my family. I'm looking forward to this visit," Vicki said as she pushed her bags into the closet.

"I'm going to take a quick shower, Vicki, and I will head downstairs."

"Okay. I will shower once you get out. You need any help?"

"Maybe after my shower, you can help me put my arm back in this sling?

"Okay, just let me know."

I quickly took out a T-shirt and some shorts, socks, and house shoes and took them and my toiletry bag into the restroom with me. I took a quick shower, washed my hair, moisturized it, and let it hang to dry.

I knocked on the door and let Vicki know that I was out and was heading downstairs.

Tania and Tasha were downstairs and had already showered and were sitting on the sofa, with large glasses of wine, laughing and talking. I smiled as I entered the room. Two more wineglasses were sitting on the table next to a chilled bottle of wine. Pouring myself a glass, I sat next to Tania.

"Thanks, y'all, for letting us come to visit."

"Girl, please, we are family, and we understand," Tania said as she patted my knee.

"What have y'all been up to? It has been too long, and I want to know what has been going on in your lives."

We chatted and laughed. I found out that Tania was a lawyer and had been for five years, and Tasha was a police officer with Atlanta PD and had been for four years.

Instantly, with the presence of Tasha, I felt safe and at ease.

Vicki came down, and I stood to pour her a glass of wine.

CHAOS

"No, Maya, sit down and relax. I can do that." Vicki smiled at me as she grabbed the bottle from my hands.

We all sat and chatted and decided to go to a club only twenty minutes from Tania's house. We all headed upstairs and began to dress.

Vicki came into my room, and she had on a nice, tight-fitting black dress and some black pumps. She had her hair down, which she never did, and it was very curly and ended in the middle of her back.

I decided to wear a sleeveless, cream-colored shirt that tied around the neck and a brown pair of formfitting slacks and some leopard-print pumps and matching bag. My hair was down and wild.

"Wow, Vicki, you never have your hair down. It's very pretty. I almost forgot you had natural hair too," I said and smiled.

"You look very pretty, cousin! Let's go party!" she yelled as we walked arm and arm down the stairs.

Tasha and Tania were down there, and they looked beautiful. Tasha was wearing a black pantsuit and some red pumps. Her hair was long and thick and cut in layers and hung down past her shoulders.

Tania was wearing a brown blouse that opened in the back, with only one sleeve, brown slacks, black pumps, and a matching bag. Her hair was cut short and in a curly mohawk.

We arrived at the club and found a table. The music was nice, and the atmosphere was pretty laid-back. All the people in there were not dressed like thugs or hookers. I looked around and smiled. The place was really high-end and very nice.

A waiter came over, and we ordered food and drinks, and we laughed, and people watched. Before I knew it, the time went by quickly, and it was 2:00 a.m., and the club was shutting down. We all decided to go to Tania's house and make breakfast.

Several men tried to approach us all night. We danced with them but never let it get any further than that. Many tried to get our phone numbers, but we successfully let them down easy.

Walking out into the parking lot, we were laughing and talking. We didn't realize that we were being watched. I had forgotten all about my troubles and had let my guard down.

As we drove out of the parking lot, a black car followed behind us. When we reached the light was when I noticed it. Every turn we made, that car made too. I quickly sobered up and sat up straight in the back seat.

"Vicki, we are being followed."

I watched her face change, and fear wrinkled her pretty face. She ran a hand through her hair and quickly tied it up into a ponytail on the top of her head. She slowly looked back, and her eyes were wide with fear.

"What are we going to do, Maya?" she loudly whispered to me.

Tasha sensing something was wrong, turned the music down, and asked what was wrong. They already knew the situation, so I told them.

"Tania, don't go straight home. Turn left up here, and do it without your blinker, and quickly," Tasha instructed her sister.

The black car made a turn with us then sped up alongside us. My heart started beating fast. Oh god, it was Daren. His sinister grin he had on his face said it all. He waved and blew me a kiss, then he veered over into our SUV, and Tania slowed down to try to avoid the blow, but to no avail.

He swerved again, making impact with us, pushing us over on the road.

"Vicki, buckle your seat belt!" I yelled as I did the same. She did as well.

Another blow from the black car, and we screamed as we took flight and the SUV flipped. It was so quick. Then there was darkness.

When I came to, it took me a minute, but I realized that I was being dragged from the SUV window. I started to scream and kick and was dropped. I looked toward the SUV and could see everyone still buckled in, but hanging upside down. I rolled over and felt pain in my legs as I tried to crawl back to them using the one uninjured arm. I saw Tania move, and she quickly unbuckled herself and pulled herself out of the SUV then began to pull Tasha and Vicki out. She looked toward me as she spoke to Tasha.

Then he was on me. "Stop resisting, Maya! I told you I was going to take what's mine. You are mine!" Daren screamed at me

CHAOS

as he stood and grabbed my arms and began to drag me again. I screamed when his hand dug into the wound he had already created.

My right leg was injured, and I couldn't move it. My left leg was just as bloody as the right, but I was able to move it a little, but not enough to get me away from him. He had the strength, and I couldn't get away from him. He was dragging me toward that black car.

"Let her go, you idiot," I heard Tasha speak calmly. I looked toward her, and she was holding her gun.

"*No*, cousin Tasha. She belongs to me," he said mockingly as he laughed, looking over his shoulder, then continued to drag me by my arm across the street.

"If you take one more step with my cousin, I will shoot you. Do you understand that?"

Suddenly he stopped, turned, and dropped me and put his hands on his hips. He let out a breath and cocked his head to the side.

"Tasha, didn't you hear me? Maya belongs to me. Why are you making this difficult? Let me have what belongs to me, and you can go on living your life. It's as simple as that!"

"Last time I checked, Daren, my cousin did not belong to you. So this is the last time I'm going to tell you. Let her go!"

Daren let out a deep breath and reached behind his back with his right hand. I didn't notice it, but he had a gun.

"Tasha, he has a gun!" I yelled.

Before he could pull it from his pants, she shot him in the right shoulder. He dropped to his knees and looked over at me. Slowly he lifted his gun toward me, and I recoiled back as I took a deep breath, waiting for the blow.

Then came another shot, this time in his chest. I heard his ragged breath as he struggled to crawl toward me, gun in hand. Again, he raised it to me, and a final shot rang out. I closed my eyes, thinking that he had shot me, and waited for my life to end. I never felt any pain and opened my eyes. He was laying on his stomach, struggling to breathe.

"I…love…you…Maya," he said as I heard the last breath leave his body, and he dropped to the ground. His eyes stared into mine. But there was no life. I didn't have to touch him to know that he was gone.

Rolling over on my side, I began to cry. I heard Tasha on the phone, calling 911. She let them know that she was a police officer, our location, and what happened.

Opening my eyes, I looked around. I felt them surrounding me. My family, Tasha, Tania, and Vicki, and I felt okay. They hugged me and sat me up after pulling me out of the middle of the street.

Looking toward Daren's body, I felt so much sadness. Not for him but for his brother, mother, and father. I was sure their loss was great, and my relationship with them would never be the same. I knew once they were told, they would mourn for him and forget about me, and it was understandable. I didn't expect them to embrace me like they did before. So much history between his family and mine—gone in the blink of an eye. I felt guilty. All this wouldn't have happened if it wasn't for me. I made the selfish decision to sleep with Daren, knowing how he felt about me. His death would haunt me, and I would have to live with that for the rest of my life. Not only had I lost a good friend but I had caused him to lose his life.

CHAPTER 14

Fresh Start

After about three weeks, I was able to return home. I had fractured my right leg, and the left was bruised and scratched. Vicki had left weeks before to return to work but came to be by my side to escort me home.

When we arrived, I was on crutches from the plane, then a wheelchair was what delivered me out to Derrick's waiting car.

I took in a breath. I didn't know what to say, and I began fidgeting in my chair once he got out of the car and came around to help Vicki with our bags. I looked around everywhere and anywhere but at Derrick. I glanced back his way; as he began walking over to me, I looked away. I was trying not to cry, but tears spilled down my face and on to my shirt.

My body shook with sobs as Derrick leaned down and embraced me then kissed my cheek. "I'm sorry you had to go through all this, Maya. We had a plan, and we wanted you and Vicki safe in Atlanta while we looked for my brother here. We still don't know how he found out where you were going."

Tears were falling fast down my cheeks. I hurt for him. He and Daren were so close, and he had to have been grieving.

Derrick's eyes got wide as he looked from me to Vicki then back to me. "Maya, what's wrong?"

"I thought you and your family wouldn't want to have anything to do with me because of what happened."

"Maya, we are the ones thinking that you wouldn't want to have anything to do with us because of Daren. We knew how he was, and we failed to alert you to the seriousness of the situation before anything happened. And for that, we hope you will forgive us. I'm speaking for Mom and Dad, and we all feel the same way."

He grabbed my hand and leaned down and gave me a big hug.

"Let me get you in the car. Can you walk, or do you need me to lift you?"

Pulling myself onto my crutches, I smiled through the tears. "I can do it. Thanks."

We rode in silence from the airport, no one talking, just the softness of Majic 102.1 playing in the background. I watched the love between Vicki and Derrick as I sat in the back seat. They were holding hands, and every now and then, their eyes would meet, and they would smile warmly at each other. I wondered if I would ever find someone. I was so tired of the games and the heartbreak. I thought of Phillip. I needed him at this moment but knew that I couldn't go back to that place between him and I. I would never be able to trust him again.

A feeling came over me. I felt guilty, watching my cousin and Derrick's display of love, and I looked away. Then I felt so much pain for me. I didn't have anyone who was going to get in my bed with me tonight and hold me and kiss away the tears. I cried softly in the back seat and prayed for some sort of relief from that pain. I asked God to send me someone who made talking to them so easy.

My prayers were interrupted by the ringing of my phone. I looked down at it and frowned. The number seemed so familiar, but I couldn't remember. Whoever it was wasn't programmed into my phone, so a name did not appear. It wasn't Phillip's; his number was still fresh in my mind. I frowned and tapped the screen to accept the call.

"Hello," I said softly into the phone. For a second, no one said anything, and I spoke again. "Hello?"

"Maya," spoke that familiar voice, then a deep, exhaled breath. "I heard what happened. Are you okay? I've been so worried, and I've been trying to call your house. My father called and told me what happened and gave me your cell number."

I sucked in a breath. I thought I would never hear that voice again. My heart started racing, and I looked toward my cousin for comfort. She was not paying attention but was engrossed in a conversation with Derrick. Part of me wanted to hang up. My stomach felt week, and my hands began to shake.

"Miles?"

To be continued

ABOUT THE AUTHOR

Ayana Williams was born in Los Angeles, California, and lived in her mom's hometown of St. Joseph, Louisiana. She moved to Houston, Texas, at the age of nine.

After graduating from Westfield High School, she joined the United States Air Force, serving six years. She holds a BA in accounting and an MBA in business with a certificate in accounting.

Her hobbies include writing, painting, baking, and traveling.

She has been married to her husband, Quincy Williams, for over nine years. She has a stepdaughter, Sanai, and a stepson, Quincy Jr., who died in a car accident in 2014.

www.ingramcontent.com/pod-product-compliance
Lightning Source LLC
Chambersburg PA
CBHW020253120125
20249CB00009B/305